It began as an experiment in temporary death. It became a spine-chilling trip into terror and Beyond, as two men battled for the woman they both loved. Stan wanted Alison. Ben wanted Alison *alive* . . .

## *LINKS*

"EXCITING . . . FRIGHTENING . . . BUT NOT EASILY DISMISSED AS 'MERE FICTION,' SINCE MUCH OF THE PLOT IS DRAWN DIRECTLY FROM MY OWN SCIENTIFIC WORK!"
—Dr. Charles Tart
Psychologist,
University of California, Davis

"THE EERIE CLIMAX WILL LEAVE READERS CHILLED!"
—*Publishers Weekly*

# LINKS

### A NOVEL BY
## CHARLES PANATI

## A TOTEM BOOK
### TORONTO

This edition published 1979 by Totem Books
A Division of Collins Publishers
100 Lesmill Road
Don Mills, Ontario M3B 2T5

The Berkley edition of LINKS contains
a different ending from the original hardcover edition.
Additional material Copyright © 1979, by Charles Panati

ISBN: 0 00 222183 7

Published by arrangement with
Berkley Publishing Corporation and
Houghton Mifflin Company

Totem Books
A Division of Collins Publishers
100 Lesmill Road
Don Mills, Ontario M3B 2T5

Printed in the United States of America

For Michael and Linda,
my brother and sister.
And, as always, for Stan.

---

With love and thanks to my Ellens:
Ellen Levine and Ellen Joseph.

Who knows that what we call death is really life, and life is death.

—Socrates

They were brothers,
   sons of *Night;*
*Thanatos,* god of death,
   and
*Hypnos,* god of sleep.

# 1

Another mutual trance was being forged.

Ben leaned back in his chair, and his shirt stuck to his shoulders. He felt calmer this week, so why was he sweating?

Alison was descending faster this time. Ben had expected acceleration with each session, but from her wilting posture he could see that this was, by far, her most rapid response. She was very suggestible. He listened to Stan instruct Alison but kept his eyes on her. Ben was the observer. An outsider.

Alison's face was peaceful, serene. No hint there of the rancor for her father or the nightmares that had plagued her since childhood and robbed him of so much sleep. For the moment, her world consisted only of Stan's commands.

At the end of five minutes, Ben clicked the stopwatch.

"Alison," Stan asked, "what is your trance depth?"

"Forty-four." A deep trance.

"Have her open her eyes," Ben said.

Stan gave the instruction.

Her pupils were dilated and her eyes watery, unfocused.

Stan stared at her. "Do you hear me, Alison?"

"Yes."

"I want you to hypnotize me. Use any technique you wish. I'll let you know when to stop." He relaxed in his chair, his hands resting on his thighs.

She was silent.

Stan repeated the instruction.

Ben played with the trigger on the stopwatch. He was squeezing the watch too tightly; it felt like a damp wafer in his palm. He loosened his grip and leaned forward. "Ask her if she understood."

Suddenly her arm rose, the index finger of her right hand almost brushing Stan's face. Though her body slouched, the finger was rigid. A comic juxtaposition. Her voice flowed, instructing Stan to focus on her finger and be fascinated by it. Then she suggested drowsiness and sleep. A light, rhythmical voice, Ben observed. More perfectly paced and modulated than when she usually induced a trance.

He made a note: object fixation; index finger right hand. He had been curious about the technique she would choose. Last week it was the ticking of a clock.

2

# LINKS

Stan's eyes closed. His mouth turned down at the corners, the muscles in his face relaxed. His breathing became sporadic, and Ben noted the fact on the yellow pad in his lap. When he looked up, Stan's breathing had slowed to a smooth rhythm, his head thrust slightly forward.

Although the tape recorder was running, Ben occasionally jotted down Alison's words. Her induction was superb, textbook perfect. Stored in her and Stan's subconscious was the posthypnotic suggestion Ben had planted early on: when he touched them on the shoulder they would hear *his* voice and obey *his* words. A simple command that gave him control.

Thirty-five seconds left. He glanced alternately at Alison and Stan. Thirty seconds. The phone startled him. He hurried across the room to his desk. Before it could ring a third time, he picked up the receiver and pushed the cutoff button. Fortunately, Alison and Stan appeared undisturbed. He was relieved. The phone was an oversight, another example of sloppiness on his part. Today was not his day. He'd left his keys in the car, forgotten to assign a reading project to his sophomore class, misplaced his latest memo to Hopkins, and now the phone. Normally he was so careful. He hoped the ringing had not obscured any words on the tape.

He opened the desk drawer and placed the receiver on a stack of uncorrected tests, then closed the drawer, pinching the coiled cord and muffling the sound. At least in the new wing of the science building, if it was ever completed, they would have modern phones with hold buttons. And warmer offices.

Returning to his chair, he touched Alison's shoulder. "I want you to stop hypnotizing Stan. Just—" Just relax, he was about to add but caught himself. Utter thoughtlessness. The instruction could increase Alison's depth. He had to watch himself. In no way, however slight, did *he* intend to deepen their trances. Only they should hypnotize each other.

Alison gazed beyond Stan or through him, an icy, vapid look on her face. Stan was totally inert. In the background, the old radiator sputtered, releasing more steam than heat. Four times a day it waged a fruitless war with the cold air eddying through the old window molding. The room was growing chilly. Being careful not to bump Alison or Stan, Ben got up, turned on the electric heater, and faced the reddening coils toward the wall so the area by the chairs would not heat up too fast.

Then Ben whispered into the recorder on his desk. "Third session. Rapid descent for both subjects. Things going better this time. Much better. Suggestibility has heightened. Remarkably so. No irregularities. So far no voice anomaly." He lowered his voice. "She had another week with no nightmares. Though other factors could account for this, such as excitement over our house... other things... general things... I believe these sessions are the major influence."

His speech was stiff, unlike his eloquent, fluid lectures. He always felt foolish talking into a tape recorder. Its circular whine seemed to order him repetitiously to fill the tape with words, sounds, sentences. To hurry and not to leave an inch of tape blank. He strained to come up with patter to please the spools.

When he finished recording, he went back to his chair. Twice before at this plateau of silence he had tried to comprehend the bond that existed between Alison and Stan. Each had focused the other's concentration, fashioned the other's reality orientation. No electric meter wired between them could measure the currents of dependency. If he told them black was white, noise was music, lemons were sweet, they would respond, Yes; white, music, sweet. And mean it! Believe it! But what greater reality would contradictions and incongruities and suggestions assume if conveyed by a trancemate? Eventually, with Hopkins's approval, he would examine that question. Alison's detraumatizing suggestions were, in a way, one small test.

Ben put his hand on Stan's shoulder, knowing full well what he was about to hear and upset that he still could not explain it. Yet he *was* calmer this week. Much calmer. Replaying last week's tape had helped.

"What is your trance depth?" he asked Stan.

"Forty." His voice was thin. Last week Alison's voice had occasionally taken on the same quality. Ben had not observed a pattern at the time, but having listened to the tape he was certain one existed. He would make sure.

"I want you to deepen Alison's trance. I will tell you when to stop."

Stan introduced a tactile sensation—her cool breath chilling her nose. He had her imagine it first, then feel it frosting her flesh, numbing her body. Suggestions of deep sleep punctuated the fantasy. Her shoulders slumped forward. The muscles around her mouth loosened, then sagged; her head tilted toward Stan.

Last year Dr. Goodman, a psychiatrist, had tried hypnotherapy on Alison after her mother's death, but with no success. Following the funeral Alison had stopped attending classes, became a recluse confined to her campus apartment, and saw no one but Goodman and Ben. And then only to cry. Neither of them could help her. Her mother was dead, making her father all the family she had. She had ignored him for years—despised him—for the agony his drinking had inflicted on her and her mother. She had such awful nightmares about him that she was often afraid to sleep. Through posthypnotic suggestions Goodman hoped to exorcise the dreams, the hatred. And, like a foreign skin graft, the treatment did not take. After Goodman's failure, Ben asked Alison to keep a dream diary, hoping that by committing the horrors to paper she might at least lessen their impact. She agreed—and also moved in with him. She improved steadily until they decided to get married, and the issue of inviting her father set her off again.

When five minutes had passed, Ben silenced Stan and solicited Alison's depth.

"Sixty-three." A very deep trance. Her voice was hollow, thin notes squeezed through a tin reed. If he was right, the mechanical quality of their voices increased with trance depth. For the next few minutes he tested their voices by asking trivial questions and by having them converse with each other. As he suspected, when they spoke to each other their voices were normal, but when they spoke to him vocal resonances vanished, tones stripped to a few frequencies. There just had to be a simple explanation for this phenomenon, which had no precedent in the literature on hypnosis. He had tried to contact Paul Pollack, his colleague and confidant, for another professional opinion, but Paul was so busy chasing women, he was rarely at home.

He had Alison increase Stan's trance to approximately her own depth, then he photographed them. Positioning himself behind Stan, he shot Alison head on. They "heard" the clicks of the shutter, Alison "saw" the flash, but outside stimuli were meaningless. He was their only link with reality. While photographing Alison, he mulled over the potential problems inherent in playing therapist with his lover-soon-to-be-wife. Loss of scientific objectivity, emotional involvement. Generally, he was able to avoid this line of thought, knowing that husband and therapist blend as smoothly as oil and water; one has to come to rest beneath the other. So far, he had managed to keep the mixture in motion. As the pictures developed detail he coated them, then locked them in his metal cabinet. Ultimately, they would be included in his paper about the project—which would make him famous.

Another week without nightmares. He concentrated on that thought as he touched Stan's shoulder. "You will relate the following words to Alison: "You have nothing to fear from your past.'"

Stan was silent.

Ben tightened his grip. "You have nothing to fear from your past."

Stan did not repeat the sentence.

"Do you understand my instructions?"

"Yes." A high-pitched, frail voice.

"Then you will repeat my words: 'You have—'"

"You have nothing to fear from your past," Stan

interrupted, his voice normal, warm, in fact. Ben frowned as he continued. "The pain and humiliation your father caused are behind you."

Sentence by sentence they ran through the litany to defuse the hatred and dispel the nightmares. Ten minutes passed. The room was freezing. The red coils shone on the wall, but their heat had little effect. Ben looked out the window. It was snowing heavily. The wind had picked up, colliding snow against the glass.

"You must not blame him for your mother's death. He loved her, and he loves you. His problem is beyond his control."

It was dark outside. Alison and Stan were reflected so clearly in the windowpane that they seemed to be outside looking in. Images in a painting, a scene suspended in space and time.

"Those events are meaningless today. They cannot harm you, or hinder your growth."

All that prevented the images from seeming a perfect portrait was the slight movement of Stan's lips. Fleeting blurs. A smear of the realist's brush. At this distance, almost undetectable.

"As you realize this, the nightmares will stop. You will sleep restfully, peacefully."

The images were in the wind, yet the wind did not scramble them. Snow blew through the portrait but did not settle on it. Their bodies, Ben thought, are shielded from the elements as their minds are isolated from emotions. He had an urge, a foolish impulse, to photograph the portrait on the window. Something was there to be captured. Understood. When he finished feeding Stan the litany, Ben placed his other hand on Alison's shoulder and addressed them both.

"Except for information you were told to remember, you will forget the events of the last hour. Your memory will be blank for that period of time. You will feel as though you have slept soundly." A gust of snow momentarily hid the portrait, but soon it emerged unaltered. "In the sessions that follow, you will obey my instructions when my hand is on your shoulder."

Instinct told him to study the images longer. There was a truth to be found in the reflection. Instead, he awakened them.

# 2

The litany did not work this time. Her tossing and turning awakened him the next morning. He glanced at the alarm clock. Six A.M.

Through the bamboo shade snow flickered and fell like jerky frames of a silent movie. He waited for her to slide under the covers, her sign that the crisis had passed. But she was motionless.

Turning toward her, he asked, "Which one, Ali?"

"Oh, Ben, I didn't want it to happen again." She was clearly disheartened.

"Honey, one in three weeks isn't bad. In fact, it's damn good." He was fully awake now. He could not, if he wanted to, go back to sleep. Alison eventually would while he lay beside her worrying, feeling helpless and defeated. What good was all his training as a clinical psychologist?

She had thrown off the blanket and was leaning against the headboard. Even in the dull morning light he could see she was perspiring; strands of auburn hair stuck to her forehead; Her legs were warm and damp as if she had been running.

"Which was it?"

She closed her black and white diary and let it drop onto the night table. "The beach with the blackbirds," she sighed in disappointment.

With herself? he wondered. Him? The sessions? "Any variations?"

After a moment of silence she asked, "There should be, shouldn't there? I mean, it'd be a sign of progress."

"Ali, let me be the judge of that. Did you notice any differences?"

"Maybe. Maybe it was less intense. Parts of it *did* seem slightly blurred." She picked up her diary to make an entry.

Had she said that to please him? Or to reassure herself? Since adolescence her nightmares had changed little. The blackbird dream was connected with her tenth birthday, when her father, in an alcoholic stupor, had caused an embarrassing scene in front of Alison's girlfriends by criticizing their mothers. Ben knew all her dreams in such detail that they could almost have been his own.

"You'd think after all these years I'd be bored beyond the point of fear," she said, more exasperated now than disappointed. He gently reminded her that subconscious events always retained their novelty, only conscious habits grew dull. Lifting his cheek from her thigh, he added, "We're doing a helluva lot better than Goodman. And it's not costing fifty dollars a week." A sum they had split for the last year.

"I know. It's just..." She fell silent and slipped down beside him.

Just what? That she was expecting too much? Perfection? But he did not probe. They *were* making progress. And another session was scheduled for that afternoon. He enjoyed holding her when she felt vulnerable. It was a sexual, not a paternal, instinct. They would probably make love soon. He thought about their upcoming wedding. At thirty-four, he certainly felt ready for marriage. Alison had not been the first woman to attract him or chase him, but she was the first to take such an active interest in his work. Her problems, in a way, had initially endeared her to him. Not long before she had teased, "If I ever become an independent person, I mean really mentally healthy, you'll stop loving me." That was not true, of course, but in mornings like this, holding her, he remembered that conversation.

By seven-thirty they were sharing the small, slanted-roofed bathroom—more like half a room in the furnished house Ben had been renting for six years. He had outgrown the house and tired of the hour commute between Boston and Ardmore. He was glad that they would be moving shortly. Shaving, he made guttural responses to Alison's questions from the shower.

Her mood had changed, as it so quickly could. The transition always amazed him. Alison Kilmore, the neurotic, twenty-six-year-old, second-year graduate student, self-named mental cripple, stepped from the shower shapely and smiling, a confident, carefree woman.

"It's bigger than we need," she said. "But you'll see, we'll fill it up. And fast."

He hoped the excitement of signing the deed would not throw off her concentration for the session. She dried herself behind him, peering into the mirror. Her hair, hands, and one hip fitted like puzzle parts around his lean frame. He thought, It's needs that really draw people together, an interlocking of needs. He needed her as much as she needed him. Her need was simply more obvious.

"Hurry," he said, slapping her wet ass as he left the bathroom, "or we'll be late."

Friday was the only day their schedules permitted them to commute together. He did not like her traveling home alone at night.

As he turned off Route 93 at the Ardmore exit, he asked her why she was so quiet. For most of the trip she had been staring at the book on her lap, twirling a lock of hair around her finger.

"No reason."

"Something's bothering you. You weren't reading."

"I was."

"Ali, you haven't turned one page."

She smiled. "Let's see the house again."

"Honey, we'll be late."

"No we won't. Not by much."

"You're not having second thoughts?"

"No! Never! I just want to see it. Please, Ben?"

He drove past the college, made two turns, then

proceeded through a maze of roads that grew narrower and more crowded with snowdrifts, roads that a week ago he had not known existed. They snaked through the woods behind the campus to Cricket Drive. Theirs was the first car to cut into the morning snow. To the right of the trees was Ardmore Lake, frozen solid; on the left were four turn-of-the-century houses spaced far apart.

"Exactly eight minutes," Alison noted as they pulled up near the house. It was the third time she had clocked the drive. She wiped moisture from the window. It was a handsome house. Imposing. Snow stuck to the old brown shingles and fattened the shrubbery around the L-shaped porch. The two-story turret contained a sitting room on the first floor and one of the three bedrooms above. On a sunny day—if another one ever occurred—light coming through the cupola illuminated the entire second-floor hall.

Alison hoped old Mrs. Wilson had finished packing. "Pull up closer."

"Ali, we don't want Mrs. Wilson to feel as if we're forcing her out. It's difficult enough for her. She's lived in that house for thirty-one years." Her husband had recently died, and she was selling the house and most of its furnishings. Ben inched the car forward, the dry snow squeaking under the tires' slow roll. He stopped by the side yard, a good sixty feet from the front porch.

"Closer."

"This is fine. You can get as close as you'd like tomorrow." He felt conspicuous sitting there at that hour, the motor idling. For the first time he realized how fast they had accepted the whole deal. Two days ago they had toured the house; today it would be theirs. He was a cautious person, slow to make decisions. It was Alison's prodding, her enthusiasm, that had sped him into the deal. He wondered what the neighbors were like. Ancient like Mrs. Wilson? On evenings when he stayed late at the college, would Ali feel comfortable in such a large, rambling house? Despite its proximity to the campus, the house was fairly isolated.

His imagination was not playing tricks on him. The curtains in the master bedroom had parted a crack. Mrs. Wilson was staring at them, aware of their purring presence, two young vultures waiting to descend upon an old carcass and pick it apart to their liking.

"Honey, let's go?"

She didn't answer.

"Ali?"

She was scrutinizing the house.

"Honey, we're late."

Alison looked back as they drove away.

# 3

The session the day before had not gone smoothly. Perhaps because of Alison's excitement over the house, or maybe Stan had had another fight with his wife, Nina. At any rate, something had disturbed their usual behavior.

Paul had at last returned, and Ben was now frantically searching for him among all the handball players down on the courts. The gym was mobbed. Too much confusion and noise. He had purposely asked Paul for a private consultation. Crossing the gym, Ben spotted Ardmore's track coach, Doc Kurcheski, a ski buddy of Pollack's. He shouted above the din, "Have you seen Paul?" With a wry smile Kurcheski responded, "Try the girls' locker room."

Dr. Paul Pollack, age fifty, had been Ben's adviser for his postdoctoral work. Dean Hopkins had paired them because of their mutual interest in hypnosis, but they had never become personally close. Pollack, Ben thought, was a brilliant researcher, but he lacked drive and ambition. Wasted genius. Or the Prodigal Pollack, as Ben eventually dubbed him. During the last few years Pollack had taken to spending a lot of time with female students at his ski lodge in Vermont. Well, Ben mused, if Pollack's going through a middle-age crisis, he's certainly having a damned good time.

Ben descended the stairs leading to the women's side of the locker room.

When Pollack had been younger and more serious, he had devoted much of his time to plenary trances, where body metabolism can slow to a crawl. He worked with hundreds of students to find the few who could achieve a plenary depth. Hopkins had told Ben about one student who sustained a plenary trance for five consecutive days. It had taken Pollack eight hours of almost constant induction to get him to that level and periodic reinforcement throughout the five days to keep him there. The student fed himself—the little food he ate—and performed necessary bodily functions, but his mind was focused on a different level of reality. Pollack never discussed the case. He had conducted at least three similar experiments with other students—all before Ben came to Ardmore. At length Pollack abandoned the experiments, claiming that they were too arduous and time-consuming, and he never published his results.

Ben found Pollack in shorts, T-shirt, and headband in the women's lounge. Pollack pointed toward the locker room. "First, I've got to get a message in there." He stopped an attractive student whom Ben recognized as a business major. "Love, be a dear and tell Dianne I have some business to attend to. I'll meet her at DuBarry's in an hour." She nodded coolly and went into the locker room. "She required a lot of tutoring last semester but didn't make much progress," Pollack said sarcastically.

They walked to the gym lobby, which was empty except for an occasional student racing through. Ben was grateful to reveal his anxiety to Pollack at last and omitted nothing. Pollack listened carefully without interrupting. The last session, Ben explained, had begun smoothly, Alison and Stan both reaching deep trances in the first volleys. "In the next five minutes, Ali's entire body melted. I had to hold her in the chair. She went from a depth of forty-eight to ninety-five."

"Did you take her pulse?" There was a doubting edge to the question.

"Twenty beats less than normal."

Pollack frowned.

"The depth is fact," Ben said defensively. "I also had difficulty believing it at first."

"Amazing if it's true," said Pollack. "Not that I doubt you, but I've spent hours getting a subject to that depth. How long have you been doing this?"

"A month."

"Nothing has ever been done with mutual hypnosis, but..." He was pensive for a moment, then he smiled. "Did her depth alarm you?"

"Not at all. If anything, it reaffirmed my belief in

the power of the technique." A plenary trance was not harmful, mentally or physically; quite the contrary, it could induce wonderful relaxation, a welcome release from stress.

Pollack pushed the wet hair off his forehead. His damp shirt clung to his chest. He still had a wiry body and was tan despite the dismal season. "You're certain of the depth and pulse?"

Was he jealous? Ben wondered. "The depth is genuine," he said firmly. "They both reached deep trances in five minutes. And plenary trances in the next volleys."

"Alison and Stan aren't on drugs, are they?"

"Jesus!" Pollack had implied that earlier.

"Just probing. Relax. With some people barbiturates can greatly facilitate trance depth."

"No, they're not on any drugs. And frankly, it's not their depths that bother me but their voices. In the last session not only did they have that metallic quality but they echoed."

Pollack leveled an incredulous stare. "Actual phoneme repetitions?"

"Yes, echoes."

"Impossible!"

"I didn't call you to argue. Their voices echoed!" Ben was aware that he was shouting and lowered his voice. "It wasn't constant, just present in a few words."

"Are you certain you weren't under some kind of spell yourself? Alcohol? Grass?"

"I'm serious."

Pollack raised his eyebrows. "So am I. The tinny voices are hard enough to conceive of. But I imagine they, at least, are possible. In a plenary trance a subject hears the hypnotist's voice as distant and hollow. Perhaps Stan and Alison were, for some unknown reason, unconsciously mimicking your voice. But an echo?"

"I taped the entire session," Ben retorted, his patience wearing thin. "You're welcome to listen any time. In fact, I wish you would."

"Well," Pollack responded, "I guess it's not physically impossible. I've heard some damn good echoes from ventriloquists. The human vocal cords can do it." He stroked his mustache. "But why? For what reason? Which words echoed?"

"I don't recall. It never occurred to me to check, but I will as soon as the tapes are transcribed." Because of Pollack's skepticism, Ben was reluctant to mention the incident that troubled him most. But he had to. After some hedging he said, "There is a bigger problem here. When I put my hand on Stan's shoulder and ordered him to stop hypnotizing Alison he didn't obey me. I kept tapping him, repeating the command, but he paid no attention."

"What did he finally respond to?"

"I shouted, '*I order you to stop*.'" In his nervousness Ben blurted out the phrase, and it rang through the lobby.

"Did he hesitate at all?"

"For a second." Ben himself now hesitated. Haltingly, he began, "The tone of Stan's last few words was, well, strange."

"Strange?"

"I can't exactly put my finger on it."

"So be inexact."

"It's as though he wanted, more than anything else in the world, to resist me, but couldn't." Ben also thought he had detected a fleeting expression of resistance on Stan's face, but he wasn't sure.

"Did you ever have similar trouble with any others?"

"What others?"

"Didn't you research the technique?"

"I didn't mean to give that impression." But he had been deliberately vague in his earlier conversation with Pollack. "I submitted a proposal. Hopkins is still sitting on it. For four months I've been feeding Hopkins memos requesting a meeting. His lack of response is beginning to drive me crazy."

"You started therapy without researching the technique and without Hopkins's approval?"

"I had no choice. Goodman was useless. I had to do something for Ali."

"And now?"

"She's fine. Much better."

It was Alison who had coaxed him to try out his theory. Hypnosis, as conventionally practiced, was an avenue of one-way rapport, one person pinpointing another's attention. Even the best hypnotist could never be absorbed with his patient as the patient was with the hypnotist. In a classroom demonstration the year before Ben had hypnotized a student while his thoughts were entirely on Alison's problems. That rote induction had driven home how extreme the one-sidedness of conventional hypnosis could be. A few days later Ben had come up with the concept of mutual hypnosis. In mutual hypnosis, rapport was balanced and total. Therefore deeper trances should be possible, Ben had reasoned, and suggestions from a trance-mate should have more impact. He'd searched the literature on hypnosis and found that mutual hypnosis had been suggested by Milton Erickson in

1933, but no one had ever really investigated the technique. That's when he devised the experiments and eventually submitted a proposal to Hopkins.

"You should have done preliminary research first."

"Ali needed help right away. And she agrees with me that I might be on the verge of some big discoveries. She argued that I shouldn't wait for Hopkins, who is obviously dragging his feet, and risk the chance that someone else might explore the same idea."

Pollack got up and walked to the front of the lobby. He opened the door and took several deep breaths. Ben suspected he was thinking about his ten o'clock rendezvous.

"Resistance is a willfull act," Pollack lectured from across the room. "It is extremely rare in hypnotic subjects." He closed the door and leaned against it, glancing at the wall clock. "If you had asked Stan to perform an act diametrically opposed to his normal behavior—killing, say—he'd resist. But your suggestion was trivial. Insignificant. There would be no reason for him to disobey." He removed his headband and tucked it into the waist of his shorts. "This thing can give you one fucking headache." He sat down on the bench next to Ben. "Did you have any problems with Stan later in that session?"

"No, none. Stan followed orders perfectly in giving Ali the detraumatizing suggestions."

Pollack suddenly gave a cocksure smile. "I think the incident was due to poor communications. Stan probably didn't hear you. Or misunderstood."

Both Alison and Stan had occasionally reacted as if they had not heard an instruction. But those pauses had been brief and hadn't bothered Ben. Stan's last delay did; something about it was different, menacing. Yet the very idea was ludicrous, contradicting every tenet of hypnosis. Ben said, "I spoke distinctly and repeated the order several times."

"All communication is based on rapport," Pollack interrupted. "The greater the rapport, the more effective the communication. As I see it, Stan and Alison were in, call it *first*-degree rapport with each other and *second*-degree rapport with you. To use an analogy, the telephone lines between Stan and Alison were clear, but between you and your subjects there was static."

"Okay, but I didn't have to shout to communicate with Alison."

"So the line between you and Ali was clear. Variability, buddy. You know how extreme it can be."

They sat in silence.

Their disagreements usually led to an impasse that ended in silence. Different silences, though: Pollack's filled with patience, confidence, and self-righteousness; Ben's with anger, frustration, or confusion. He always came around to Pollack's point of view. Pollack was always right. Ben had to admit that Pollack's logic was sound. Theoretically, there should be a difference in rapport. He liked the terms first- and second-degree rapport. Had he read Stan's tone incorrectly? Had he let emotion cloud his observations?

"Could differences in rapport have a bearing on the voices?" Ben asked.

Pollack shrugged. "Who can say? If the channels of communication are different, why not the voices that come over them?" Again, he looked at the clock. "Invite me to a session sometime, but right now I've got to shower and dress."

Ben threw his coat over his shoulder and followed Pollack across the lobby. "How about this Friday?"

"Can't. I'll be in Vermont."

"I'd like you to hear the tapes."

"Sure, but not this week."

"I hoped we could discuss your work with plenary trances."

Pollack seemed amused. "Ben, buddy, you probably know more about it than I do."

"Did you keep notes?"

"I tried not to."

"Nothing?"

"Not unless I was careless and jotted something down."

For all the good it would do, Ben asked, "Would you look for them?"

At the door to the locker room, Pollack extended his arm in a gesture of futility. "I wouldn't know where to begin."

"You promise to sit in on a session next week?"

"Right on."

Ben left through the back entrance. The night was clear and cold. He inhaled deeply. First- and second-degree rapport. Very clever. Clever indeed. Despite Pollack's predictably smug attitude, Ben felt more confident, partly due to Pollack's calming, logical evaluation and partly due to sharing weeks of observations with someone—anyone. Wasn't that what he advised his patients? Open up, talk; you'll be surprised how much better you'll feel.

# 4

The house legally belonged to them, but Mrs.
Wilson still hadn't moved out. Each day for over a
week she had telephoned, profusely apologetic; she
had underestimated the task of packing, and the
movers could not accommodate her delays. The
recent snowstorm had kept the local firms she'd
called from taking on the job. But she would leave
soon, very soon, she promised.

"You should insist," Alison scolded Ben after the
last phone call. "It's our house. We'll never get it
fixed up before the wedding."

"Ali, we're not getting married until Easter
recess."

They were dressing to go to the Frederickses' for their usual Wednesday night dinner together. These weekly dinners, which alternated between Nina and Stan's and Ben's houses, became a custom shortly after Alison moved in with Ben. For Alison, they broke up weeks that were heavy with dull lectures, weeks in which she often wondered if she would have remained in graduate school so long if she hadn't met Ben.

"She's only asking for a few more days," Ben added, pulling on a blue crew-neck sweater. "It's not like we're left out in the cold. We can stay here for another two months if it comes to that."

Alison slipped into a pair of brown slacks and a beige jersey top and sat at Ben's desk brushing her hair. "You should have asked how soon was soon," she said into the mirror she'd propped up on the desk. She would have to revise her plans for cleaning, painting, rearranging—everything. Priorities would have to be shifted. The permutation of possibilities cluttered her mind. She brushed her auburn hair forward, letting it fall over her shoulders, framing her chiseled features. It was an exquisite face enlivened by green eyes and a smattering of freckles, a face that sparkled when she was excited and assumed an enticing sexuality when she pouted.

"It's not fair to us," she said, "or legal. We could force her out."

"Jesus, Ali, that's a rotten thing to say! Mrs. Wilson is going through a tough period in her life."

"I was just thinking out loud." She got up and tucked Ben's shirt collar under his sweater and gave him an offended glance. "You needn't take that seriously," she said as she went downstairs.

Ben was not concerned about Mrs. Wilson or the house, for he was preoccupied with a strange feeling he'd had in the shower. And curiously, that feeling made him apprehensive about seeing Stan at dinner. He flashed on Stan's voice on the tape and his resistance to following instructions. During his shower he had actually hallucinated Stan's face, the image so vivid it had frightened him. A residual unpleasantness lingered still. Ben puzzled over the fact of his uneasiness; more than a week had passed since that troubling incident. The most recent session had gone perfectly. By speaking loudly and distinctly, as Pollack had suggested, there had been no hitches. He'd phoned Pollack to thank him and was so relieved that even Pollack's "I told you so" attitude did not irk him. The echoes had been present again but were fainter and totally random. Why then this fear? And tonight of all nights? What had triggered it?

On the way downstairs he felt a strong urge to share this incident with Alison, but to do so would violate his own rule that they not discuss the sessions. Personal feedback would interfere with the therapy—and the experiment.

In the foyer, helping Alison with her boots, he wished he didn't have to spend the evening with Stan.

But the hour's drive had a soothing effect on him, and the Frederickses' wine and good dinner eased him into an amiable, even jocose mood.

Stan and Nina lived in a two-room apartment about a mile from campus. Stan had taken the apartment in his sophomore year when he married Nina, a petite, energetic blonde a year younger than Alison. At the time, Stan worked part-time in the Ardmore library and Nina was a reporter for the *Mystic Gazette,* a local paper. Now that Stan was working feverishly to finish his dissertation by June, Nina's salary was their only income—a touchy issue between them. Her dinners for Ben and Alison were simple but always excellent. This time, however, she had gone all out.

"It's a celebration," Nina explained as Stan placed a glistening roast goose on the table. She lit two red candles and placed them on either side of the platter. "For the new homeowners." During the meal Alison dominated the conversation with her plans for the house.

"If only she remembered classwork with this detail," Ben interrupted Alison's enumeration of the qualities of the house.

"You've got to motivate her," Stan responded. "A little behavioral conditioning. A gift for every *A*." He rocked back in his chair, balancing on two legs, grinning at Ben. Like Pollack, he had a cocky smile. "Well, mentor?"

Ben and Stan enjoyed a relaxed, informal relationship. But since Ben had become a "couple," he and Stan had grown even closer.

Ben laughed. "Will you pay for the trinkets?"

"With what?"

Ben caught the tense expression on Nina's face. He was about to change the subject when Alison said, "We're recruiting you both to help us move. You"—she pointed at Stan—"for the heavy stuff."

"Soon, I gather."

"Yes, soon. Very soon. That's a promise."

"I'm dying to see the house," Nina said, placing a bowl of lime sherbert covered with diced apples, oranges, and nuts next to Ben. "Maybe I can do an article on it. Joe goes for architecture and renovation pieces."

"You won't like it," Stan said.

"Why not?"

"Not your style." He turned to Alison, his naturally ruddy complexion flushed red from the wine. "Strictly modern; she's all for practicality and minimum upkeep."

"He's teasing," Alison said.

"It's true," Nina said, "but I can appreciate old houses, too."

"Baby, the first thing you'd do is replace the shingles with aluminum siding."

Alison laughed as Nina twitted Stan, "I'm practical, but not tasteless."

Ben slowly twirled the stem of his wineglass. "You've seen the house?" He was certain Alison had not mentioned the shingles.

"I drove by. I'd hate to mow that lawn! How many acres?"

"Three."

Alison reached across the table for the dessert bowl, and her elbow tipped her wineglass. Rosé wine fanned out across the Formica tabletop, spilling onto her slacks and the floor. "How clumsy," she apologized, blushing, dabbing at the wine with her napkin. "I'm awfully sorry."

"Don't be," Nina said, already down on her knees and sponging the linoleum. "In this place, nothing can get damaged."

Stan went to the bedroom and returned with an old pair of slacks. "Here," he said, tossing them to Alison, "put these on and let Nina soak out that stain."

Stan went into the kitchen to plug in the coffeepot. Ben picked up the signs that Alison had had too much to drink: her flushed face and that cat-sly grin. When Stan brought in the coffeepot, Ben poured her a cup.

"Drink this. You'll feel better," he said as she returned to the table in Stan's baggy khakis.

"I'm fine." She giggled.

"Ali."

"No, Ben, it'll keep me up tonight. I'm not drunk. Really." For everyone's amusement she walked one of the wavy lines in the linoleum pattern. "See?"

They stayed until eleven, later than usual. On the way home, Alison raved about how much fun Stan and Nina were. She was drunk and leaning against Ben's shoulder. On her lap she held their first housewarming gift, a conically shaped decanter and four footed blue liqueur glasses. "They're really wonderful. Nina's offered to help me as soon as Mrs. Wilson leaves."

# 5

The foyer was long and poorly lit, as musty as the rest of the house. On both walls above the dark mahogany paneling were ornately framed mirrors six feet high that reflected against each other. The foyer reminded Alison of an old movie theater. Ahead and to the left were bare wooden stairs to the second floor; to the right, the hall narrowed considerably and the dark burgundy carpet grew thinner and more frayed as it passed the paneled dining room and stopped at the swinging door to the kitchen. Alison and Nina entered the living room through tall mahogany doors.

"I can walk into the hearth," Nina said, an

exaggeration because at five-foot-two she was more than a foot taller than the opening. Running her fingers over the spotless baby grand she sighed, "It's in mint condition. Shame no one plays." After Alison showed off the house, they began cleaning.

Ben and Alison had finally gotten Mrs. Wilson to move.

Alison had come across an ad for a moving company in Nina's paper. The snow didn't bother them. She had cursed herself that neither she nor Ben had looked in the newspaper sooner. Mrs. Wilson was delighted, and on Wednesday afternoon they carted away her things. That evening she boarded a bus in Boston that had by now deposited her at her daughter's home in Johnstown, Pennsylvania. The next day, despite classes, a howling wind, and the first signs of a head cold, Alison met Nina in front of the house at nine sharp. "Wait until the weekend," Ben had said when he awakened. "We'll start moving in together." But how could she possibly wait? How could he expect her to? She had to get rid of her nervous energy. She'd awakened twice that morning not from nightmares but because she was so eager to get started.

During breakfast Goodman had called, and that upset Ben. "What did he want?" Ben asked when Alison returned to the kitchen.

"Nothing."

"He called for a reason."

"He called to find out how I've been feeling lately, and I told him I'm fine and that I've had fewer nightmares. I didn't mention the sessions."

"He must have been curious. Nightmares just don't suddenly stop. Not after all these years."

"Maybe he didn't believe me."

32

For the first time in their relationship, she suspected that Ben felt she was hiding something from him. He looked as if he wanted to ask why Goodman was pursuing an ex-patient. Ben's silence made her feel guilty, and after Ben left for Ardmore she sunk into a mild depression. Later, working in the kitchen of the new house, she realized she had overreacted. Surely Ben accepted Goodman's call for what it was: a doctor's concern.

"You clean with a vengeance," Nina observed. "Would you care to do my place next?"

"I'm enjoying this. It's relaxing."

"Relaxing? Boring or time-consuming, yes, but hard work is never relaxing."

"It's a contradiction, I realize, but that's how I feel." Her fever and the throbbing in her head did not diminish her drive.

Nina watched in amazement as Alison began throwing away dishware. From her mother Alison had learned that a hairline crack in a plate or cup served as a nest for deadly bacteria. No detergent or water temperature was strong or hot enough to kill the germs. Over Nina's protests, Alison threw away four bowls and cups, two plates, a serving platter and three dessert dishes, silverware that was bent or badly scratched, and glasses that did not pass her rigorous scrutiny. What remained she dumped into steaming water along with pots, pans, and cooking utensils.

"Jesus! I've got to take a break," Nina said, staring at the tall glass doors of the cupboard that was her next task. She sat down at the kitchen table. "Is there any chance of getting a free cup of tea for the help?"

"Sure, just a sec."

Alison went into the pantry. Alone in a room of the house for the first time, she delighted in a new sensation: a private communication between her and her home. Until moving in with Ben, she had never lived in a house, only a string of apartments. As her father changed jobs and relocated the family, she changed schools and friends. Ben's house, although rented and abominably furnished, had given her a sense of self and place that she relished. She had been impressed that a house—without noisy neighbors on the other side of the wall—could provide so much peace and stability. Those same feelings washed over her again, soothing her, but more intensely.

"Ali! Have you fallen into a canister?"

Nina's question snapped her out of her reverie. Had she known she would have preferred being alone in the house, she wouldn't have accepted Nina's offer. She found the tea bags, boiled water, and while Nina sipped the tea, Alison washed the dishes in the sink. She resented Nina's griping. Nina had volunteered, after all.

By midafternoon her cold was worse and her head ached, but Alison refused to quit.

"You're going to kill yourself," Nina snapped.

"It must be ready before the wedding. It *must* be ready," Alison said sharply.

In silence they cleaned out the upstairs closets, piling cracked plastic coat hangers, frayed and stained towels, faded sheets and pillowcases, and a collection of men's clothes in the hall.

"You're not throwing this stuff away?" Nina asked incredulously.

"Take anything you like." Alison instantly

regretted her supercilious response but did not apologize. Her headache was almost unbearable.

"That's not what I meant," Nina responded. "Send this stuff to the Salvation Army. It's a tax deduction."

They started on the closet in the guest room. Alison figured the chill she felt was due to her fever but noticed Nina examining the window frame.

"It's freezing in here. Must be coming in from the top," Nina said. The window extended high above her reach. "Ask Ben to seal it. It'll make a big difference."

Alison was relieved when Nina went home to prepare dinner.

Alison felt much better the next morning and cut classes again to drive to the Lindencrest Mall for their January white sale. Walking through the mall's glass-enclosed, tree-lined center, she passed a music store and on impulse wandered in. She suprised herself by buying a beginner's book on piano instruction. "With a baby grand in the living room it would be a shame not to learn how to play it," she said to the sales clerk. Her last stop was at a plant store, where she bought two ferns, a hanging fuchsia, some bird's-foot ivy, and her favorite, a gardenia plant.

Leaving the mall, she had every intention of meeting Ben for lunch, but as she approached the campus her desire to spend time alone in the house became irresistible. Nina's presence had ruined the day before.

Hanging her coat in the brass tree in the foyer, she decided that Ben would understand when she explained at their four o'clock session that she had wanted to do more work in the house and so skipped their lunch date. It was almost noon. In four hours she could accomplish a lot, but she'd have to keep track of the time. "God," she said aloud, "he'd never forgive me. Lunch, yes, but a session, no way!"

She placed the ferns in the living room by the french doors to the porch, hung the fuchsia in the dining room window, and put the ivy on the windowsill in the kitchen. Locating the jar of instant coffee Nina wouldn't let her discard—"It hasn't been opened, Ali. No germs could have gotten in"— slit the paper disk and boiled water. Without cream or sugar the coffee was bitter, but she soon forgot the taste as she thumbed through the piano book. "Tarantella." "A Frolic in Velocity." "Wrist Staccato." *Habañera. March of the Gnomes.* Skimming over the "Barcarolle" from Offenbach's *Tales of Hoffmann,* she figured it would take years to learn to play.

Taking her coffee into the living room, she sat at the piano. It was a cloudy day, but when the sun broke through, light glistened off the silver and gold wires inside the piano. As she hit the keys, she watched the wires shimmer in the sunlight, each losing its substance to become a humming blur. Alison was intrigued. She stood up and struck a chord. How beautiful! Wires vibrated, fattened, divided into doubles, triples—endless, infinite multiples of themselves—then merged. Every wave of sound carried directly to the center of her head and sent out concentric, overlapping rhythms that resonated through her body. Relaxing, warming waves.

# LINKS

Alison stood motionless, her eyes unfocused, unaware that the chord had stopped vibrating ten minutes before. Suddenly she grew aware of her position. Frowning, she instinctively scanned the piano's interior. What had she been looking at? Or for? She shrugged, sat down, and, curious, studied the key placements in the piano book. Then she tried various pieces at random. To her amazement she was not terrible, not nearly as bad as she had expected. Delighted at first, after practicing for an hour, she then felt strangely uneasy over her progress. The association between notes and keys had been almost too easy to remember, and apparently she had an uncanny ear for melody, for once into a phrase her fingers usually landed on the correct keys. Her hands seemed at times to have a will of their own. She stood up, closed the keyboard cover, and laughed at the thought that she might be a latent prodigy. A closet clavichordist. But her stab at humor did not dispel her queasy feelings.

Alison washed her coffee cup and went upstairs to put sheets on the beds. In the guest room she stepped back to admire the elegance of the canopy bed. "Ben will just have to get over the claustrophobia of sleeping in a canopy bed," she said with a smile, determined to have it moved to the master bedroom. She shivered, thinking, Jesus! Nina was right. The cold is worse in here. Standing on a chair, she felt along the top of the window. Nothing. Where was the damn draft coming from? Poor insulation? Well, kiddo, you bought an old house, you asked for this. Chalk up one hidden cost. As Alison fitted the bottom sheet to the mattress, a piece of wood underneath caught her eye. A plywood board. That's why the bed was so firm. After Nina had gone, Alison had taken a nap on top of the bed and slept more soundly than she had in a long time.

She set the gardenia plant on the table in front of the window. At various times in her life she had had gardenia plants but could not coax them into blossoming. She equated her own stunted and fragile growth with the sensitivity of the flower and its continual need for attention. At Ben's house she had failed to lure white petals on two plants. She misted the new plant. Maybe the room's cool temperature and southern exposure could change her luck.

Alison glanced around the room. It was filthy! God, where to begin! The cleaning involved overwhelmed her, and she felt very tired. Ben liked her to rest before a session; it helped her concentration. She pulled back the new sheets and climbed into the bed. She loved the snug security the canopy created. The draped roof enclosed her, protected her. She would sleep well in this bed. But not just then. She would just relax until the time for her session.

# 6

Ben checked his watch. Alison would be worried that he hadn't arrived yet, and Stan would be somewhat concerned. Already he had endured an hour of rambling conversation with Hopkins about school politics, tenure, raising graduate requirements, and gossip—everything but his project. He was hot and irritable. It had not been a good day. He was glad when Mrs. Bruckner broke in on the intercom; "The architects are on the way over."

Hopkins yelled at the intercom, "Tell him to go to hell." His loud, abrasive tone surely cut through the closed door.

Hopkins was a bearish man with improperly

proportioned parts: a head too big for his body, a nose too big for his face, and a bulging stomach too heavy for his thin legs. Ben had learned from experience not to interrupt, cross, or contradict Hopkins. When he addressed you, you graciously accepted the honor and listened. And listened.

Hopkins eased his cumbersome body into his desk chair. "They're killing me," he said gruffly. "I curse the day I agreed to oversee the renovation." They were off on another tangent. Ben poured himself another cup of coffee. It only made him sweat more, but his frustration had worn down his common sense. Go with him, he advised himself, it had taken long enough to get in to see Hopkins.

"You're going to resume the renovation?"

"West, at this point I don't know if the school's going to continue. No, I retract that, but quite a few people won't continue next semester."

"Staff?"

"Of course staff! Those asshole students represent income. Some of the staff have to leave." He laughed coarsely and cleared his throat. "But that's not your concern." He began rummaging in the stack of papers on his desk.

Ben finished his coffee. He felt tired. The whole day had been frantic. Hopkins's cordial note—"See me at 2:30"—had raised his spirits after Alison had not shown up for their lunch date. But he worried about her, and then Mrs. DiVetto had telephoned to say there was a constant hum on the tapes. They weren't ruined, but the hum was annoying and drowned out the softer parts of conversations. Too embarrassed to explain the source of the hum, Ben promised her cleaner tapes in the future. He cursed himself for not putting the telephone receiver in the bottom drawer of his desk instead of in the drawer directly beneath the recorder. Wood was a good conductor of sound.

"You think it'll work?" Hopkins asked, leafing through a copy of Ben's proposal.

"I believe so."

In the six years he had been a professor at Ardmore University, he had published over a dozen papers on the use of hypnosis to break the habits of compulsive smokers, eaters, and alcoholics. Suggestions of aversion coupled with convincing motivation was the routine formula. It worked, but only with a small number of people, and the effect was not permanent. He was certain that he had devised a technique that would not only break habits but be powerful enough to cope with more complex problems, such as Ali's. The proposal outlined two years of experimentation that he was eager to begin.

"Suggestions in mutual hypnosis are more effective?"

"That's what I want to investigate, sir. Ninety percent of the population is hypnotizable, but only about ten percent can experience profound trances. Mutual hypnosis might greatly inflate that number." In the proposal, besides a subsidy, Ben had requested that his teaching load be cut by thirty percent and that he be assigned the services of a full-time research assistant.

"How accurate is this depth scale?"

Despite Hopkins's bland tone, Ben had the impression that Hopkins was more pleased than he let on.

"Amazingly so. Once a person's taught the

divisions from zero to one hundred, and the corresponding symptoms, the answer comes automatically. It's standard."

Hopkins stared intensely at Ben, his bushy eyebrows bunching together. "How deep? And how fast?"

Ben was gratified that Hopkins was familiar with his material and seemed to be approving the project. "Sir, I can't say. No one can. That's the purpose of these experiments." Did that sound flippant? Since Erickson first recommended mutual hypnosis in 1933, only three papers on the subject had been published, and none of them really probed the potential of the technique. "I intend to go beyond the published research on the depths, the speeds, the results." But he wasn't ready yet to confide his initial discoveries to Hopkins—not until Pollack helped him solve several problems. If Hopkins continued to question him along these lines, he would have to lie. He couldn't jeopardize the project by Hopkins's finding out that he hadn't researched his technique and was having trouble with Stan.

Hopkins waited for Ben to explain the project in more detail. Ben shifted in his chair uneasily, then began, "The depths will vary depending on the pair of subjects, the number of volleys, and the duration of each one." No dishonesty there. Ben discreetly looked at his watch. Ten after four.

"Is there any danger that two subjects could get locked in a mutual trance?"

"No danger at all," answered Ben, smiling. "At worst, if a subject gets too hooked on the trance fantasy, he or she eventually will drift into natural sleep and awaken." Alison would be nervous. It was unlike him to be late. She would be speculating with Stan: a car accident, a fight with a student. Whatever, it would be like her to assume the worst.

Impatient, Hopkins hunched over his desk. "Accurate, I'm sure, but uninformative. With money as tight as it is, I can't go to the Board and argue for subsidizing this research on the basis of such a general prospectus. They'd kick my ass out, and fast. You can't just tantalize them with speculations, not when things are so bad they didn't even grant themselves a raise this year." He pushed himself out of his chair. "Nevertheless, I like your idea. I'd hate to see Ardmore lose it because some boob at an Ivy League school publishes first."

Ben was confused. "Sir, are you telling me to go ahead?"

"I can't do that. Not without their holy sanction. But you're a licensed psychotherapist and have your own clients. If, *on your own time,* you could prove to me that your confounded scheme works, provide me with impressive ammunition—and I mean *hard figures*—then I'll go to bat for the funds."

The lampposts around the quadrangle shined into Hopkins's office, and the conversation of students headed home, finished for the week, was another reminder of the time. Present time. Passing time. This late time of Ben's life, his mid-thirties, when, if he was going to make his mark, this was *the time.* Why not? What did he have to lose? Exploring a theory without proper supporting research could cause a scandal, but on the other hand, this was his big chance to make a name for himself. He would need Alison and Stan's approval, but he knew they would give it willingly. Alison certainly appreciated his ambition. He'd be recognized as a pioneer in the field of mutual hypnosis, an international authority on the subject. The sessions with Ali and Stan would be the pilot study to win Hopkins's approval and the Board's. Even at this early stage, the results were impressive enough. A smile spread across Ben's face. He would give Hopkins more material but would withhold selective information. No need to disillusion Hopkins with paradoxes that would soon be resolved.

"Okay, Dr. Hopkins," Ben said, standing, "here goes."

# 7

Stan and Alison were sitting in their chairs, knee to knee, when Ben walked in. Alison was laughing about something and seemed anything but concerned about his late arrival. Ben was hurt. She apologized about not showing for their lunch date and explained that she spent that time working at the house. Lately it had seemed her only concern, and he was beginning to feel jealous. For a year he had been the center of her life, but now he was competing with a house for her attention. Ben did not show his annoyance as he didn't want to ruin the session. Instead, he got it under way immediately.

They went under fast, incredibly fast. After

months of hypnotherapy some patients have only to lie on the psychiatrist's couch to pass into a light trance. Stan and and Alison's response was a great intensification of that phenomenon.

Alison was at a depth of sixty-seven; Stan, seventy-two. Such deep trances in five minutes were unheard of! Had their body physiologies not shown marked changes, he himself would not have believed it. He recalled Pollack's comment that there's always the possibility he lucked out with two subjects who happened to be highly suggestible and ideally matched, but he had noted an unmistakable ring of jealousy in the remark.

Carefully Ben had observed Stan hypnotize Alison. After two minutes her breathing had become labored. Stan had seemed intrigued by this but unconcerned and hadn't broken his induction. When Alison reported her depth, Stan hadn't flinched. In each session, Stan watched Alison go progressively deeper on the opening volley.

Ben circled the chairs as he shot photographs from several angles. He coated the pictures and locked them in his cabinet. Standing behind Alison, he placed his hand on her shoulder. "Alison, you hear my voice. How do you feel?"

"Very calm. Content. I am floating, but my body is very heavy." Her voice had that cold, mechanical tone. And a slight ring, but no echo. Its faintness made him turn toward the desk, but this time he had remembered to wrap the phone receiver in a towel in the bottom drawer. With his other hand on Stan's shoulder, Ben reminded himself to speak distinctly, clearly.

"I want you to deepen Alison's trance. I will tell you when to stop."

Stan did not hesitate. "We are at the entrance of a long cave. We are beginning to go inside. You can see the walls."

The induction startled Ben. Descent into a cave, down a flight of stairs, rope, or ladder, was a common and effective technique. But they hadn't used it before. Ben listened raptly to the elaborate details of the fantasy. Stan described a long, wide cave, inky black at its entrance and vibrantly bright inside. Cavernous walls glistened yellow and white, illuminated by a light from a source far ahead. Alison and Stan did not walk, but floated past shimmering figures of other, unidentified people. No effort was required to move anywhere in the cave. Beyond, the cave's walls refracted the white light in a rainbowed spectrum. A silvery mist coated the cave floor.

Stan led Alison past each feature, having her concentrate on them one at a time. Oddly, he did not mention drowsiness or sleep, yet Alison's response was profound. There was no discernible muscle tone in her face, and she looked younger than her age. Then, as the seconds passed and her skin softened more, she grew older. Her skin sagged. Her body seemed to melt like a waxen figure in a blistering summer sun. Her upper torso bent forward, jeopardizing her balance. Gently Ben leaned her against the back of the chair. The cave excursion was rapidly deepening her trance.

Stan's explicitness astonished Ben; he was so vivid and precise that Ben could almost visualize the cave himself. Where, he mused, did Stan find the mental energy, the ingenuity, to construct such a fantasy?

Stan's voice was melodious. Mesmerizing. Literally mesmerizing. Ben realized that there was a danger in listening too attentively. He had often hypnotized an entire classroom of students with the right words and tone.

Ben counted Alison's respiration rate. Six breaths per minute. Pulse twenty-five beats less than normal. Her whole physiology was slowing.

After four minutes and thirty-five seconds, something peculiar happened. Stan cautioned Alison about a brilliant spike protruding from the cave ceiling. A few seconds later her head jerked to the right, and she squinted as if at a blinding light. To her, the cave was totally real. She was living the adventure. A perfect hypnotic subject who accepts the trance world as the only world, the only reality.

The expression on Alison's face was one of utter peace, accentuated by the paced, slow breathing of deep relaxation. Absolute tranquillity.

In the middle of Stan's description of a colorful rock formation, Ben touched his shoulder and spoke loudly and firmly, "I want you to stop hypnotizing Alison."

"The rocks run on to the left and lead to a stream—"

"I *order* you to stop hypnotizing Alison."

"The light will not bother you if you—"

*"Can you hear me?"* Ben yelled. It was impossible that he was not getting through to Stan.

Stan continued, his voice warm, encouraging.

*"You cannot disobey. I order you to stop!"*

Defiance flashed across Stan's face. His forehead tensed, his nostrils flared. He had heard Ben, there was no doubt about that. Ben checked his watch: twenty seconds too long. He shook Stan violently.

*"I order you to stop. You will listen to me. You must."*

Again, Stan's defiant expression, yet not a trace of anger in his voice, which was rhythmic, inviting. Ben was sweating and agitated. *"Stop! I demand that you stop."*

"You hear music up ahead. We could—"

Music! He was engaging her auditory sense. A deliberate act. It had to be. An attempt to increase the cave's reality.

Thirty-six seconds too long. Ben's mouth was dry; he had a hard time swallowing. His hands clung to Stan's shoulders, shaking him in the chair. He had to get through to Stan. *"You cannot disobey. You—"*

Suddenly Alison's body fell forward. Ben caught her. She was so pliant, flesh without bones.

Stan's voice ran on, lyrical, intoxicating—and calculated! Impossible as it seemed, Stan was defying his instructions. This can't be happening, Ben said to himself, trying to fight his panic. Sweat poured freely down his face, and the blood pounded in his ears. As he watched Alison sway forward, an idea occurred to him. Sitting her upright in her chair, he said, "Alison, I order you to obey. You will insist that Stan stop hypnotizing you this instant."

"Stop." It was all she uttered.

Stan was silent.

Ben shivered with relief. He had not realized how cold the room was. It was freezing. Pressing his hands against his legs, he closed his eyes and worked to control his breathing. He felt as if he had run for miles and been stopped abruptly by a brick wall.

When he opened his eyes, he noticed Stan's

childlike expression. The dark sexuality that was legendary on campus and had attracted so many women had disappeared. Alison's head tilted to the left; she seemed so peaceful. Ben let them rest until his racing heart slowed to a more normal rate. He yearned for commotion in the hall, any noise. Students arguing or laughing. But all he heard was the steady whir of the tape recorder. He did not try to unscramble his thoughts. He couldn't for the moment.

Six minutes and eleven seconds had passed since they had hypnotized each other. He had to know. Gingerly he rested his hand on Alison's shoulder. "What is your depth?"

"Twooo huuundreed and teeen...and teeen... and teeen...and ten...and ten..."

The echo filled the space, bouncing from every corner, surrounding him as though it emanated from a thousand sources scattered around the room. The echo rang painfully in his head. He realized he had to control himself. He breathed deeply. Two hundred and ten! He had to make sure it got on the tape. Again he asked, "What is your depth?"

"Twooo huuundreed and teeen...and teeen... and teeen...and ten...and ten..."

At last the sound faded away. It was inhuman. Fearful of continuing, Ben terminated the session. He placed his hands on Alison and Stan's shoulders and suggested that their trances would lighten as he counted down from ten to zero. To his relief they awakened readily when he hit zero. He wasted no time in removing his hands from their shoulders. He didn't want either of them to detect his trembling.

# 8

Ben was not sure what he was looking for, but he'd been watching Alison closely all weekend. Maybe an expression, a word, some telltale sign, any hint that might indicate her recollection of the awful session.

Alison drained grease from the bacon and lined the strips neatly by the eggs. She buttered the toast, mixed the orange juice, and set the food on the table. Perfectly normal behavior. All weekend she had been ebullient about their moving.

"You feel better?" he asked, closing the box of tools he would take to the new house after breakfast.

"Much better. I just wish I could shake this cold." She sat down at the table, and he joined her. "This is our last meal together here."

"You've been working too hard, Ali. We can't finish the house in a few weeks. It's old, it needs repairs and refinishing. It'll get done in good time." He tried not to sound pedantic, which she had accused him of the night before.

"Ben, I'm fine, and my appetite is back."

She did look better and had more color in her face.

"You will call Nina?" he asked.

"It's light packing. I can do it myself."

"I want you to call her," he said, reaching across the table to put his hand on her arm, a gesture intended to lend force to his words. "Nina offered. Take her up on it."

"She's helped enough already. I really hate to ask again. And there's not that much left to do."

"Ali, do me a favor. Please."

She looked down at her plate.

"Promise me you'll call Nina."

Reluctantly she agreed.

After breakfast, she handed him a list of things to be done at the house.

"Whatever you and Nina don't pack, I'll finish tonight," he said on his way out.

Ben took advantage of the morning sun and unseasonably warm temperature to work outside on the back door, which did not lock. Once the frame was sanded, then the door itself, he chipped off the layers of paint coating the hinges and clogging the latch. The physical work was a relief. Since Friday he had been brooding over the failure of the session, and his uncertainty and anxiety festered in him, building up an intolerable pressure. He had to confide his fears to someone. Twice he had phoned Pollack, who was no doubt sunning himself on a ski slope. Ali was out of the question, of course, and discussing the session with Stan would ruin the experiment. Anyway, what could he say that would make any sense? The impossible had happened, and who would believe him? He wondered if his choice of Stan as Alison's partner had been a mistake. Stan was highly competent, that's why he'd selected him, but maybe his chemistry with Ali was *too* strong.

Ben gave up on the broken branches, bricks, and assorted debris in the back yard; snow still covered too much of the ground. He was oiling the hinges of the french doors, which opened only with force, when he heard a car start in the driveway of the adjacent house. He trotted around the porch and down onto the front lawn, hoping the driver would see him and stop to talk. He could use some company. But the car, a silver Mercedes, had already turned into the street. Hoping someone else would appear—it was such a beautiful day—Ben worked for the next hour in front of the house, replacing the molding along the porch roof that the movers had accidentally dislodged. Only once did he go inside, and that was to dial Pollack's number.

Shortly after one, Ben was resting on the porch, eating the lunch Alison had packed for him and trying to relax and enjoy the day, when he heard a car coming down the street. He walked quickly down the flagstone path to the front pavement, his half-eaten sandwich in one hand, a warm beer in the other. Cricket Drive was not long, and he instantly recognized Stan's brown station wagon.

"This is certainly a surprise," Ben greeted him.

Stan leaned out the window. "You're loitering on your own sidewalk it seems." He parked in the driveway.

"I thought it might be the neighbors."

"Is she that interesting?"

Ben laughed. "That's what I'm investigating."

While he showed Stan the house, he analyzed his feelings. He'd actually been shocked by Stan's arrival, but then the shock wore off and was replaced by a curiosity over his behavior.

"What do you think of this old house?" Ben asked.

Stan smiled broadly. "I think I'm going to get rooked into working my tail off."

Ben was tempted to ask if Stan had expected to find Alison there. But the question was so blunt that he knew it would sound asinine.

They rearranged the living room furniture according to Alison's diagram, placing the faded burgundy sofa opposite the fireplace and arranging the chairs and table around the sofa. In the dining room, they moved the rectangular oak table away from the wall and into the center of the room. It was a heavy piece, and they grunted as they lifted it. They placed the breakfront against the wall. Both of them were breathing heavily. Ben caught his breath as he mulled over the questions he was eager to ask Stan: Why was he here today? Was he looking for Alison? Ben observed nothing unusual in Stan's behavior, and by the end of the afternoon he was embarrassed at having been unprofessional enough to let his imagination prejudice his relationship with Stan. Stan promised to help him move the last things into the house that evening.

Ben returned home to pack the remaining cartons with his personal records. He was flabbergasted by the sheer quantity of school papers, lectures, tests, and notes of experiments he had accumulated. What a packrat he was! On the bedroom floor he sorted and filed them into labeled boxes. The research he had done for the Boston police, and published, was the most fascinating.

As he was about to close one box, a report caught his eye, a case he had worked on two years earlier. The body of a forty-one-year-old woman had been found lying in the living room, naked, stabbed several times in the chest and thighs, and raped. The woman's six-year-old son was found crouched at the head of the stairs. The police were convinced that the boy had witnessed at least some part of the murder and could help identify his mother's assailant, but the youngster was in a catatonic state. Ben had been brought in to hypnotize the child in order to communicate with him. He was easy to hypnotize, and, once he was under, Ben nudged him back to the night of the murder. Eventually he had provided a complete description of the murderer and part of his threatening commands.

Ben pondered the last page of the report. The murderer had been a Southerner and the boy a New Englander, but under trance he related the man's words with a southern accent and in a voice more husky and mature than his age. Was there a clue here, Ben wondered, a clue to the voices in the sessions? Or was he groping anywhere and everywhere for answers? Maybe Pollack was right, that Ali and Stan were mimicking Ben's voice, the way it sounded to them. If so, though, why? And why would his voice have an echo?

"Don't read them, dummy, pack them." Alison leaned against the door, smiling. "You're never going to finish at this rate."

Ben carried the cartons downstairs. The hall was lined with shopping bags, suitcases, boxes, and pillowcases stuffed with odds and ends. "With our two cars and Stan's station wagon, we'll make it in one trip."

But by eight o'clock the Frederickses had not arrived.

"When Nina left, she said they'd be back no later than seven," Alison said. Getting edgy, she went through the house again, checking drawers and closets. "I don't appreciate this. Of all the times to be late."

"I'll call again." Getting no answer, Ben shrugged. "We may as well start packing."

They loaded the two cars and stacked the last cartons near the front door. "There's not much left over," Ben said. "Maybe we could squeeze them in." A good deal had to be unloaded in order to pack more efficiently. They worked fast, and to prevent Alison from sinking into the depression beginning to overtake her, Ben reminded her of their anticipation of being settled in the house and the renovation they planned, all the things she wanted to hear. They managed to pack all but four boxes of books.

Just then Stan and Nina pulled up in front of Ben's car. They apologized, not looking at each other, through clenched teeth. It was clear that they had had a fight and were not speaking to each other.

Two hours later, all the cartons had been carried into the foyer of the new home. Nina and Stan had barely been civil. Ben knew of an all-night pizza place and offered to treat everyone. "We have wine here, if I can figure out which carton it's in." Alison volunteered to pick up the food. "Take Nina," said Ben, sitting on one of the cartons, winded. He did not wish to be trapped alone in the tension between Stan and Nina. From past experience, he knew it could be stifling.

"No, I want her to supervise with the draperies."

Alison was out of the house before Ben could remind her how late it was and that the draperies could wait. He shrugged. "I don't want to disappoint Ali, so I guess I'll start on the curtains."

"You're certainly considerate of Alison," Nina snapped, glancing at Stan.

Ben went upstairs to get away from Stan and Nina, but they followed him. The draperies were the same blue-gray fabric as the canopy on the bed. Standing on a chair, Ben began hanging them in the master bedroom. Stan stood on a chair to help.

"The curtains are too short," Nina said. "Let me see if there's a hem."

"Ali found these in a closet. They'd been cleaned, but maybe they're meant for the window in the guest room."

"I think there's enough of a hem to let out."

Stan scowled. "Alison probably wants them this length."

"They should just break on the floor." Nina was determined to have the last word.

Ben stepped down off the chair. The uncomfortable situation reminded him of their summer vacation on the Cape. Nina and Stan's continual bickering had ruined the two weeks.

"When you move the canopied bed in here," Nina said, "this place is going to resemble a period room in a museum."

"Ali's gotten the notion that the bed is elegant. I'd just as soon get rid of it."

"I don't blame you," Nina sympathized. "It's a foreboding piece of furniture. I sure wouldn't care to sleep in it."

"No one asked you," Stan said.

"I'm talking to Ben."

"Baby, the bed they sleep in is their business."

"At least they sleep in the same bed," she retorted, leaving the room.

"Are you moving the bed now?" Stan asked.

"God, I hope not. I'm bushed." From the window, he saw Alison parking in the driveway. Apparently the move had not tired her. She practically ran to the porch with the two boxes in her arms. Her enthusiasm over the house delighted him, though he was still annoyed with her for cutting classes to work on it. Now that they had moved, he thought, he'd have to be firm about priorities.

Alison came into the bedroom. "The grub is in the kitchen. I didn't bring it up here because I don't want stains on the carpet. The curtains look terrific, but they're too short. Good, there's enough hem. Where's Nina?"

"Slow down," Ben laughed. "She's somewhere downstairs, I guess. Let's eat. I'm famished." As they passed the guest room, Ben asked, "You really want this bed moved tonight?"

Alison stopped at the doorway, Stan directly behind her.

"It'll be a helluva job taking it apart. I don't know where to begin, and I'm damned tired. Can't it wait?" When Alison didn't respond, he added, "But if you and Nina remove the bedspread and sheets, I'll..."

The bed was magnificent, yet for the first time it seemed frightening. She was drawn to it, but it also repulsed her. What was her strange fascination with the bed? It was pretentious, not elegant. Her energy seemed to drain away. Her ambivalence over the bed started a buzz that settled around her ears and throbbed painfully in her temples. She was caught in a conflict, torn between vague alternatives that could only be defined in terms of the contradictory emotions they stirred in her—fear and calm. The room turned cold. So cold. Didn't they feel it? Surely Stan felt it. He was close behind her. Coming closer. Touching her, his breath an icy vapor on her neck. A hazy fear kept her from approaching the bed. Like a daydream displacing reality, the bed consumed all of her concentration.

"Ali, what's wrong? Come on, honey, don't sulk. I'm joking. Of course we'll move the bed. Right this minute."

"No, leave it here."

"I wish you meant that."

She turned to him. The chill disappeared. "I do. Leave it in this room—permanently."

# 9

Hopkins beamed at the report on his desk. He'd been thinking over West's project during the weekend, getting increasingly excited about it. He went to his office on Sunday to reread West's proposal. MacPherson's memory experiments with rats four years before had been the last project to spark his interest to this extent. Hopkins had gotten a lot of mileage from MacPherson's research, and he anticipated far more publicity from West's.

He played with the figures, subtracting one from another, juxtaposing them, making comparisons and estimates, and at length he plotted a curve of Induction Time versus Trance Depth. The red dots assembled into a partial pattern, one that invited inference, begged to be extrapolated. He connected the red dots with black ink, and a wavy curve climbed high and away from the Time axis. He loved fiddling with figures. Hard numbers.

How much of the experiment should he reveal now? And to whom? He wouldn't, of course, jeopardize the work in progress by prematurely publicizing it. But he sure as hell did not intend to be completely close-mouthed about it, either. Not with this hot property. To his faculty he would praise West's research as an example of excellence, a level of originality they should all be striving for. He would use it to light fires under them. But his greatest pleasure—he leaned back in his chair and smiled—his greatest pleasure would come in hinting to Shaffer at Columbia and Brinkley at Harvard that Ardmore was sitting on something hot. Tease them green. Goad them on. And when West's paper was published, he would flaunt it in their faces. Ardmore may be a small school, he thought pridefully, but it could compete with the best of them.

Hopkins picked up the report. Damn stimulating stuff. His mind raced. Before he started bragging, though, he'd better clear up a few points with West. Why, for example, stop at four volleys? Why not eight? Or twenty? Were twenty volleys possible? For how long could one volley continue? And why use only two people? How about four? Or ten? A circle of subjects. Intertwining inductions. Webs of subliminal connections. A network of minds interdependent and finely tuned to a highly formidable, amenable mentation. Was this a

first-order approximation of Jung's collective conscious?

West was doing great work—for starters. But his
report was sparse, incomplete. It contained no
explanations. He needed figures *and* flesh. Where's
the flesh? Hopkins wanted blood.

# 10

Ben had to talk to someone or he would bust. All day Wednesday he rang Pollack's number, getting more frantic as the day wore on. At length, a woman answered. She was obviously angry that Pollack hadn't shown up.

"Do you have any idea when he'll return?" Ben persisted.

"Listen, if I did, would I be hanging around waiting like a damn fool?"

"When you speak to him, please tell him I've been trying to reach him. It's urgent."

"I'm not gonna stick around much longer. Just tonight."

"But you will leave my message? It's awfully important."

"Sure, if he comes soon. But don't count on it. I'm not."

Ben thanked her and hung up. The afternoon light, eclipsed by the west wing of the building, was fading from his office. He unbuttoned his gray cardigan and stared blankly at the papers on his desk. Maybe it had been a mistake to include Ali in his experiment. Had he already lost his objectivity? And where the bloody hell was Pollack! He'd promised to sit in on a session and help him. The pressure of not being able to cope with Stan's defiance was getting to Ben.

Ben focused on the problem at hand: Friday's session. There was no getting around it, he'd have to cancel it. He couldn't continue until he spoke with Pollack, found some answers. The door opened, and Alison breezed in.

"Shall I wait for you? I can study in the library until you're ready to leave."

"Would you mind?"

"Not if you don't mind eating late."

"Not at all. I won't be long. Stan and I have to discuss some organizational problems with his dissertation, then we can go."

"Okay. Ciao."

"Ali? Just a minute." He decided to tell her then. "Honey, I'm afraid Friday's session is off." A bad opening, too blunt; he saw it in the expression on her face. "Skipping a week won't make any difference. We're doing fine."

"But why? I really depend on the sessions. They're helping me a lot."

Ben concocted an excuse on the spur of the moment. "Hopkins has scheduled a meeting with me. You know, one of those rare honors that no one dares pass up." He had never lied to her before, and he hated himself for doing it. Yet he couldn't afford to tell her the truth because it would jeopardize the experiment. "Ali, you won't even miss it. Trust me." He put an arm around her shoulder. She shrugged it off. "Honey, what's wrong?"

"I had a nightmare last night."

That startled him. She looked away.

"Why didn't you wake me? Or mention it at breakfast?"

"Oh, Ben, it was horrible. The falling dream. I was going to tell you tonight."

Her evasiveness upset him. "Honey, you're not making this up, are you?"

She was genuinely hurt. "How could you even think that?"

"I'm sorry." He hugged her. "Ali, the excitement of the house, the novelty, the disruption of moving—all of it can throw things off. It could be responsible for your nightmare. In fact, canceling the session might be a good idea, to gauge how well you're doing on your own. Maybe you're becoming too dependent on therapy. It might be wise to spread the sessions farther apart."

"I'm not ready for that yet," she said earnestly. "I was counting on the Friday session—especially after last night."

"Don't deprive her of it," Stan said, peeking in. "Am I interrupting anything?"

"No."

Stan walked over to Alison. "Is he giving you a

hard time?" he joked. "He's been giving me a hard time, too, bullying me about my dissertation. Are you really canceling the session, Ben?"

"I'm afraid I have to."

"Do you think it's smart to disrupt the weekly pattern we've established?"

"It's not," Alison answered. "A certain regularity is important."

"Hey," said Ben, careful of the tone of his voice, "hold on a minute. I'm in charge here. Besides, you two aren't supposed to be discussing anything whatsoever relating to the therapy. Nothing."

He turned to Alison. "Honey, I'll meet you in the library. We'll continued this on the way home."

As she retreated down the hall, Stan slid into a desk seat. His dissertation had been separated into three piles. Ben became the teacher once again. For the moment at least, he was in charge.

# 11

Alison spent Friday morning in bed, propped up by pillows and reading, attempting to please Ben by catching up on her courses. Her cold had gotten worse during the week, but finally her fever had broken. She felt her forehead. Cool. Her appetite had decreased, her stomach was somewhere in her throat. Her illness was psychosomatic. She admitted it. Patients get anxious, often hysterical—they develop blisters, warts, rashes—when their psychiatrists take vacations. She was well aware that therapy could be as addicting as heroin and the withdrawal as painful. She was an apt student of psychology, human behavior, and the mind, but she could not apply her knowledge to help herself.

At ten o'clock Dr. Martha Swope, the university physician, arrived. Because Ben had sent her over, Alison submitted to the examination. She coughed on cue, stared at Dr. Swope's hairline while a light probed her pupils, stuck out her tongue, gagged, crossed her legs which jerked normally when Dr. Swope tapped them with a hammer, shivered at the touch of Dr. Swope's icy hands probing her breasts, had her temperature taken.

"I told you you wouldn't find anything," Alison said, putting on her bathrobe. "It's all in my head."

"Dear, most disease is. But the physical symptoms can be very real. You're rundown. I want you to stay in bed today and rest over the weekend. Monday, come by for a blood test."

Alison did not protest, and Dr. Swope let herself out.

Alison awakened around noon feeling less wretched. She remembered her promise to call Father O'Rouke, the pastor of Saint Sebastian's Church, and dialed his number from the extension phone at the head of the stairs. She *was* feeling stronger and less apprehensive about the canceled session. The line was busy, so she dialed again. On the way to the university she had passed Saint Sebastian's, but not until a few days ago had she given it a second glance or considered having a church wedding. Alison had not been in a church for ten years, and she felt strange in Saint Sebastian's. She assumed she had not made a good first impression on Father O'Rouke. He was pleased that Ben was Catholic, but surprised that she had not yet discussed a church wedding with him, and of course he was disturbed by her admission that they had been living together.

"You and Mr. West have been living as husband and wife for a year?"

"Yes."

"You'll both have to receive the sacrament of penance, you know."

"I've been away from the sacraments too long, Father. Can you hear my confession now?"

"I'm afraid not, Ms. Kilmore. If you come back on Saturday or during any mass—Easy there. Let me help you. You'd better sit down for a while. Are you all right?"

"Just a little weak."

She had sat in the church for half an hour, until the dizziness subsided; then she had practically coerced Father O'Rouke into hearing her confession. She had driven home feeling greatly relieved yet puzzled by her intense urge to get back into God's good grace.

After her third try, she went back to bed, waking at three. Her forehead was cool, and for the first time in a week she felt hungry. She inspected herself in the bathroom mirror. Her eyes seemed clearer, and she satisfied herself that she was recuperating. She washed her face and, sitting on a stool by the bathtub, brushed her hair.

The yellow stains mottling the tub bothered her. "It's age, not dirt," Ben had said. "If it really upsets you, I'll coat the tub with white epoxy." Dirt or age, the marks were ugly. Perhaps Nina hadn't scrubbed the tub hard enough. Alison took a can of cleanser and a sponge from the closet behind the bathroom door. She splashed water into the tub, then scattered the cleansing powder from end to end. It fell like snow, white and pure. She sprinkled more powder and watched it drift downward, coating the yellow stains white. Everything white. White ceremony. White dress. White lights. Rows of white gardenias. White altar. White runner down the aisle.

Her reverie was shattered by the phone's ringing. Grudgingly, she stood up and went to answer it. But before she could reach the phone it stopped ringing. No doubt Ben was checking to see how she felt. She would call him after she finished in the bathroom.

She paused in the doorway of the guest room, the one room she and Nina had not cleaned. The bureau was covered with dust, and with her finger she drew a circle in it. The floor and bookcase were also dusty, as were the night tables flanking the bed. One of the night tables was blemished. She rubbed at the hard, sticky substance and smelled the wood. The scent was medicinal. She surveyed the room. It pleased her that the gardenia plant had sprouted buds, and on two of them the waxy green coverings had peeled back to reveal white layered teardrops. Getting her equipment from the bathroom, she watered and misted the plant. She loved the fragrance of the flower. She sniffed a second time and inhaled a raw green odor. It would take a lot of time and work to fix up this room, which badly needed painting and replastering on walls where nails had held pictures. She preferred white to the pea green color of the room. For her wedding the church would be white and the altar lined with white flowers. Her daydream was again interrupted by the phone. She picked up the receiver, but there was no one on the other end.

She returned to the guest room and scraped at the stain on the night table with her fingernail. She knew she was procrastinating. Cleaning to avoid studying and writing her father. She'd promised Ben she would drop him a note, but she had successfully avoided doing it all week. Write to him now, she ordered herself. She sat at the desk in the room that was being transformed into Ben's study and wrote a perfunctory letter. Date, time, place, new address. An impersonal letter. She couldn't recall the last time she'd communicated with her father. At her mother's funeral, she'd barely acknowledged his presence. She was deciding how to sign the note when the doorbell chimed.

As she opened the front door, Stan walked in, thrusting a present at her.

"Another one?" She was surprised to see him.

"A small and selfish housewarming gift."

"You've already given us one."

"Well, here's another. You'll understand when you open it."

They went into the living room. Stan had bought a heavy yellow marble ashtray, rough-hewn around the rim and highly polished in the center.

"Since you're the only one of the four of us who smokes, where would you like it?" Alison asked.

"You don't mind it in the living room?"

"Why should I? It certainly won't encourage Ben or me to smart smoking, if that's what you mean." She smiled. "At least now you won't be flicking ashes into my cups and saucers." Placing the ashtray at one end of the coffee table in front of the sofa,

Alison suddenly felt very self-conscious. She shrugged off the feeling, readjusted the ashtray, and, looking up, found Stan staring at her.

"Ben said you were sick, but you seem fine to me."

"Now, yes. But for the past several days I've been feeling lousy."

He continued to stare at her. She slid the ashtray to the middle of the coffee table.

"I'll break it in," Stan said, lighting a cigarette and sitting down on the sofa. "From Ben's description, I expected to visit a gray ghost of a woman. You're completely recovered."

Still he stared. She forced a smile and pressed her hands awkwardly against her hips. Her hands felt cold, and she sensed a numbness in her legs. Was she having a relapse? she wondered.

"It was sweet of you to come over," she said, sitting in the chair next to the sofa, not knowing what else to say. Why was she so nervous with Stan, of all people?

"Don't overdo it," Stan advised. "Ben mentioned how preoccupied you've been with working on the house."

Why was he staring at her like that? An answer sprang to mind, but she instantly dismissed it. Surely Stan knew better that to discuss the sessions with her. It was one of Ben's cardinal rules. Anyway, what was there to say? She remembered nothing of them.

"Would you like something to eat or drink?" she asked abruptly.

"Do you have any fruit? An apple?"

She took an apple from the refrigerator and

washed it. The cold water ran over her hands for a long time. Her fingers began to sting. She remembered as a child being warned to keep her gloves on in the winter and that it seemed easier to make snowballs, build snowmen, without them. She turned off the spigot and laid the apple on the counter. The throbbing began behind her eyes and spread to her temples. A dull drone. She did not want to face Stan, but she wasn't sure why. Solitude was what she desired just then. Talking to Stan seemed so difficult, so exhausting. Slowly, she dried the apple and put it on a plate.

Stan stood in the doorway. "Ali, are you all right? You look faint."

"I'm fine. Here."

Stan sat down at the kitchen table. He stared at her.

It took a great effort for her to speak, but she finally managed to stammer, "I must start dinner."

"Please, go ahead. I wouldn't want to be blamed for Ben's starving."

With a concentration intended to conceal her nervousness, she unwrapped a capon and sprinkled it lightly with paprika. Why, in God's name, am I shaking? She washed and dried a head of lettuce and quartered two tomatoes. All the while, Stan rattled on. Occasionally she glanced his way to show she was listening, but she couldn't hear him over the pounding in her ears. Was she going crazy? She seriously began to wonder. For the last few days she'd been beset by unnamed fears and the rumbling in her head. She knew she was neurotic—Dr. Goodman had made that plain enough—but was she crossing the line into psychosis? Now that she had fewer nightmares, was the poison inside her venting itself in her waking hours? Did it still need to be released? She'd have to talk to Ben; she couldn't hold out any longer. Either this was a reaction to the canceled session or the therapy was ineffective. She hated to hurt Ben's feelings or drop out of the experiment, but she obviously needed help. Her symptoms were characteristic of a flight from reality, escape. But escape from what, exactly? Maybe Ben's therapy was only superficially effective. She prayed that that was not true, for she felt she'd rather die than shatter his dream.

Stan stood up, and walked toward her.

"Ben should be home any minute now," she said. "I can't imagine what's keeping him." She wanted to move away from Stan but her legs seemed paralyzed.

"Ali, what's the matter?"

She barely heard him through the buzzing in her ears. She nodded, thinking, He's concerned. I'm ill. I look terrible. That's all. Yet she wanted to ask him not to come any closer. She wished Stan would leave her alone. Suddenly she blurted out, "Ben canceled the session, not me."

"Ali, I don't mind the cancellation. Are you on any medication?"

She forced out the words. "I'd like to lie down."

He followed her into the hall, his eyes burning through her back. "Will you be okay until Ben gets home?"

"Fine." It was hard to form words. She was weak. Smile, she thought.

"If it would help, I'll stay until he arrives."

Shaking her head no, she smiled and opened the front door.

"Damn, it's raining. Listen, Alison, relax. Get some sleep. I'm concerned about you."

She closed the door, leaning against it for support. Her head felt as if it had split open and a fine mist was painfully oozing out. The buzzing increased, and the room grew dark. Her body trembled. She slumped to the floor. Oh God, God, don't let Ben find me here. What's happening to me?

# 12

Ben switched off the tape recorder and stood by the window. The snow had turned to icy rain. Alison was expecting him, but he would not cut short his meeting with Pollack now that they had been able to get together at last. Pollack, sitting on the edge of Ben's desk, had listened to the tape in silence, his face blank.

"Did you photograph Stan?"

"The camera was the farthest thing from my mind. All I could think of was to stop him!"

"Funny, the tone of his voice doesn't even hint at resistance or aggression."

"I told you that. We went through that before you heard the tape."

"Calm down. I'm merely puzzling over the facts out loud. That's all."

Pollack had been impressed by Alison's depth of two hundred and ten. He figured Alison must have been aware of some internal body rhythm, her heartbeat or something much subtler, to estimate the depth. A combination of physiological effects. The body is composed of clocks.

Pollack moved to the desk chair. "I still maintain that you can't rule out Stan's expression as one of personal pain or anguish. Some incident from his past might have triggered his reaction." He looked at Ben. "You know why surgeons aren't permitted to operate on their wives?"

"Jesus Christ!" When Pollack got hold of a theme, he kept repeating it.

"I know how objective you are," Pollack said, "but one of your subjects happens to be your fiancée. That can easily taint your observations, or your interpretation of them."

Ben fumed. "If you insist on carping about my objectivity, there's no sense continuing this discussion."

Pollack was silent for a moment. "Do you agree that at Stan's depth he could have seen or felt something frustrating or painful from his past? That your grip on his shoulder suggested an unsettling memory?"

"If you'd been there," Ben answered, "you'd feel differently."

"*Feel* differently?"

"Okay, *know* differently."

"Then, Professor West, you develop a line of reasoning."

"Assume that my interpretation is correct. That Stan deliberately resisted my orders, that he continued to hypnotize Alison of his own volition. Given those conditions, what explanation can be deduced?"

While Ben talked, Pollack sorted through the photographs of the session.

"Nothing there," Ben said, annoyed.

Pollack divided the photographs into four rows of three each, then rearranged their order. "We tend to think of particular states of consciousness as all-or-nothing affairs. A person is either awake or asleep, hypnotized or not hypnotized, drugged or sober. However, mixtures occur, and in far greater or stranger combinations than we imagine." He held up a picture. "The configuration of the three chairs is highly informative. An excellent blend—whether you realize it or not—of experimental design and purpose. Form and content. In this picture, the experimenter is and is seen to be an integral part of the experiment. Physically and mentally." He handed the picture to Ben. "Stan and Alison are linked to each other through their mutual trance, and you are linked to them by your implanted posthypnotic suggestion. I venture to surmise that each subject experiences a split state of mind. Part of Stan's hypnotic consciousness is focused on you, part on Alison."

"Two streams of consciousness operating independently yet simultaneously. Yes," Ben considered. "I remember reading about a hypnotized subject who was made to listen to two different taped conversations, one played in one ear, one in the other, at the same time. The subject heard both conversations and wasn't confused by the experiment. Such cases are rare, but there are precedents."

"One of the most common examples," Pollack said, "is the lucid dream, where the individual is living the dream and is at the same time aware that it is only a dream. In fact, he is sometimes aware of being in his own bed in his own home. A blend of dream consciousness and wakefulness coexisting independently and harmoniously. It could be that Stan and Alison possess functional vestiges, however small, of wakefulness."

"Through me?"

"Through your participation in the hypnosis. Don't forget, in conventional hypnosis a very small percentage of people can learn to integrate wakeful reality into profound trances. Of course they have to be trained to be active somnambulists, and they need help in reintegrating wakeful standards. It doesn't happen spontaneously. And it only occurs in extremely deep trances. Usually, as soon as you attempt to have subjects make strong contact with wakeful realities, they automatically wake up." Pollack selected two more photographs for Ben. "Mutual hypnosis is such a strange bird. You might be experimenting with a mixture of hypnotic consciousness and *active* wakefulness."

Ben stared out over the dark campus at the lights around the library and, on either side of the building, at the woods extending back to his house and the lake. He should phone Alison, he thought; she might be worried that he'd be late, but he wasn't in a particularly considerate mood. Pollack's doodling on the cover of the college telephone directory was reflected in his office window.

"How long have you known Stan?" Pollack asked.

"Six years. Why?"

"How do you evaluate your relationship?"

"Very friendly."

"That's it?"

"And very informal. We see each other socially at least once a week, and we've planned vacations together."

Pollack drew concentric circles around the college logo, idly adding radial lines. "Has there ever been friction between you and Stan?"

"No. None at all."

"Does he harbor any hostility against you? Maybe latent hostility?"

"None. I say that with confidence. And I consider myself an astute observer of human behavior."

"As his mentor, you do, to a large degree, influence his future. For instance, in your accepting or rejecting his dissertation and in your providing the recommendation essential for his landing a decent teaching position."

"Every professor has that kind of control over his students. We're all under someone's thumb."

Pollack glanced up from his drawing. "Is Stan in love with Alison?"

"Alison and I are about to be married!"

"Congratulations. But I repeat, is Stan in love with Alison?"

"Absolutely not!"

"Alison is a beautiful woman, Stan is a sexy guy. God knows enough girls around here flirt with him."

"They are good friends." Ben was shouting.

"Period. If Stan were after Alison, I'd have detected it. When Stan's interested in someone, he's anything but subtle, believe me."

"Relax. Hang loose, as my latest love says. I'm following *your* line of reasoning."

"Besides," Ben said, in a tone meant to squelch the issue, "he only ogles blondes."

"True. He's consistent there."

Ben had a sudden urge to call Alison, but Pollack continued. "Frankly, there's no need for all this fuss. If I were in your shoes and had enough ambition, I'd be overjoyed. Whatever the reasons—and there must be good ones—you've achieved plenary trances in a matter of minutes. You've got yourself a unique and enviable situation to explore. One that will generate a hell of a paper. And that's just the beginning. So you run into a few anomalies, a few blind alleys. What researcher worth his reputation doesn't? Buddy, the milestones come from solving puzzles, not avoiding them." He stood in front of Ben. "Tell me—and I demand an honest answer—tell me you would be this upset if the subject were not Ali but a student volunteer."

Ben walked over to the chair just vacated by Pollack and sat down. Then it dawned on him, why hadn't he realized it earlier? Maybe there was a way to unravel the paradoxes, or at least shine new light on them. The sessions were designed to be perfectly balanced, calculated to be mutual between the subjects. Yet Alison and Stan's behavior was not identical. Only Stan presented a problem. In the hypnosis protocol, one factor was glaringly out of sync, but he could manipulate it. Pollack stared at Ben, expecting an answer.

Ben articulated his new insight. "Stan has always led each session. He induces Alison's trance while fully awake and he watches Alison submit to his influence. Alison has never witnessed her influence on Stan."

Pollack grinned. "Intriguing observation. That's the analytical Benjamin West speaking. Well, there's only one way to test its significance."

Ben collected the pictures on his desk.

"You're not giving up, are you?"

"No." Ben hesitated. "The therapy is obviously benefiting Alison. Anyway, she'd be furious with me if I did. She had a fit when I canceled today's session."

"When is the next session?"

"Anytime next week. Whatever day you can be present."

"Friday's okay by me."

# 13

Alison awakened to find herself lying on the floor in the foyer with no recollection of what had happened. She was relieved that Ben had not discovered her that way; he hadn't yet come home. But she couldn't remember being so scared. Something was definitely and seriously wrong with her, and she couldn't keep it to herself any longer. She'd obviously lost control and needed help. She decided to call Dr. Goodman first thing on Monday after she got to the campus. If she was lucky, he'd let her come right by.

She got through Saturday all right but had another "attack" on Sunday. After Ben had left for

Boston she had practiced the piano, and the next thing she remembered was hearing Ben's car. Three blank hours had flown by. Repeatedly she reminded herself that she mustn't panic, that Dr. Goodman would straighten her out. She dared not confide in Ben. She had formed the words in her head but could not bring herself to confront him with the truth—or one possible truth—which would be devastating. His mutual hypnosis, his pride, joy, and professional vehicle for success, was a great failure. It had not exorcised her nightmares, but merely suppressed them, channeling the old hatred and fears, the childhood traumas, into an unconscious flight from reality—hallucinations, fugue states, dissociation, the whole classical repertoire of symptoms. The sessions worked but at the expense of creating new problems.

She felt strangely calm on Sunday night, once she felt that she knew the truth. But the clear light of morning brought confusion. Suppose her neurosis had evolved into psychosis. That would at least explain her desire for the weekly session, for they represented hours devoid of problems and anxieties, a respite from recognizing how sick she was becoming.

Alison entered the student union and made her way through the snack bar, hurrying but trying to appear relaxed. In the hall she caught her breath and regained her composure, then slipped into a phone booth. The dime clinked, and she dialed the number she knew by heart.

"Dr. Goodman's office—"

"This is Alison Kilmore."

"Dr. Goodman is not in right now. This is a recording."

"Damn."

"At the sound of the beep please state your name and leave a brief message and a number where you can be reached. You have one minute. The office reopens at two o'clock."

One minute. A brief message. How could she possibly condense all she had to say, all her confusion, into a few words. She felt betrayed. When she heard the beep she involuntarily covered the mouthpiece with her hand, as if her thoughts, in unstructured fragments, might escape into the receiver. She had spent much of the weekend arranging and rearranging those thoughts to get a coherent picture of what had happened to her, *was* happening to her and growing worse.

Discouraged but determined to call back, she returned to the snack bar. On a speckled plastic tray she placed silverware, a cup of clam chowder, and a small dish of cottage cheese that she didn't want and poured herself a cup of black coffee. It was her first meal in twenty-four hours. Ben had been chiding her lately for being distracted and having no appetite. He was clearly worried about her.

Alison was inclined to sit by herself but joined three classmates instead and halfheartedly added to their conversation. It helped; she felt better. Conversation and activity ameliorated her headaches. Daydreaming and idleness, she'd come to realize, were dangerous. When her mind was not engaged it drifted into vague reveries, then blankness. She forgot fragments of days. Hours vanished beyond recall.

After her two afternoon classes, in which she could not manage to concentrate, she went back to the student union and called Dr. Goodman.

"Yes, Alison Kilmore. I used to be a patient." The voice was unfamiliar.

The receptionist said, "I see that your last appointment was December seventeenth. You'd like to resume weekly visits?"

"No, I just want to see Dr. Goodman for one appointment."

"Dr. Goodman does not believe in single visits. Nothing can be accomplished in an hour."

"This is not for therapy. I simply have a problem—a personal problem—and would like to confer with Dr. Goodman."

"All Dr. Goodman's patients have problems, and all their problems are personal."

Another student occupied the phone booth next to Alison, and she lowered her voice. "I must speak to him. Tell him it's Alison Kilmore. He'll talk to me."

"Ms. Gilmore, Dr. Goodman is on vacation."

Alison felt as if she'd been doused with a bucket of ice water. "When is he expected back?"

"Monday, a week from today. But he's not accepting appointments his first day in the office."

Alison forced authority into her voice. "Tell him Alison Kilmore will be by Monday at noon."

"But—"

"Thank you." She hung up. She'd have to wait a week; she had no choice. Keep busy, that's the secret, she reminded herself. Surround yourself with people and chores. A week isn't that long. But as she walked past the snack bar she admitted to herself that next Monday seemed a light year away.

"I might as well be chairing a faculty meeting,"

Dr. Hopkins said as Alison ushered him through the crowd.

"Ali, the house is great."

"Terrific, Ali. Seth and I gave ourselves a tour. However did you find it?"

"Luck," she shouted above the commotion. "Plain luck."

"Any new blood coming?" Hopkins asked, picking at the assortment of food on the dining room table.

"It just so happens there is. The couple in the next house and the widow at the end of the drive."

"How old?"

"About sixty-five."

"Don't introduce me."

The doorbell rang, and Alison excused herself. She looked radiant in a beige crepe dress, her hair pulled severely back at the sides. She passed Ben chatting with two professors by the fireplace.

"Honey, do we have any more lighter fluid?"

"In the pantry. Second shelf."

She opened the door and greeted Professor and Mrs. Loren and hung up their coats. The professor mumbled about the cold weather, and Mrs. Loren exclaimed, "Dear, this is priceless. How old?"

"Sixty-eight years, according to the realtor." Alison was surprised that the compliments on the house meant so much to her.

"Ali," Nina asked, "should I bring out the other ham?"

"I'll do it."

"Nope. You've been racing around like crazy. Enjoy your own party."

"Is Stan coming?"

"He might drop over, I'm not sure. He's hard at work on his dissertation and is getting nervous that there's so little time left."

There was a burst of applause in the living room and, turning, Alison saw the fire blaze in the fireplace. Ben admired the spectacle as if he had just discovered fire. He was thoroughly enjoying himself. Initially he'd been opposed to the party because it entailed so much preparation, but her insistence plus the promise to keep it small—which she did not do—had paid off. The planning and shopping had kept her occupied, and she had survived—and without incident—three days of the light year.

Opening the door again, she guessed that she had overestimated the Rogerses' ages by ten years. They were Ben's age and lived next door. Katherine was a lawyer and Patrick owned a chain of dry cleaning stores in the Boston suburbs. Mrs. Blum, the widow, was right behind them. "It seems like yesterday I was here." She extended her hand to Alison. "Wonderful people, the Wilsons."

"Yes, they were." Then she realized she'd never met Mr. Wilson and was about to amend her answer when Mrs. Blum said, "Tragic, grotesque death. Such a pity. He was such an energetic man."

"Grotesque?"

"Yes, cancer. A long-drawn-out fight."

"Oh, well." Alison shrugged. Mrs. Blum frowned in disapproval. "I'm sorry," Alison said. "Of course it's tragic. But I thought you meant he had some awful accident."

Mrs. Blum looked at her gravely. "All death is grotesque."

Alison regretted inviting Mrs. Blum. "Old crow!"

she said under her breath. She caught up with the Rogerses.

"I hope you can't hear this racket next door."

"Quite clearly," Patrick said, smiling. "Every word. That's why we decided to come." Alison liked him.

Katherine asked, "Is it you who plays the piano?"

"I play at playing. I'm teaching myself."

"Don't be so modest. From what I've heard, I'm impressed."

Alison introduced them around. Mrs. Blum hovered nearby, and Alison settled her on the sofa, then went to check things in the kitchen.

"So you're doing something important in hypnosis research," said John Pool, dean of the business school and one of Ben's regular tennis partners.

"How did you know?" Ben was irritated.

"Hopkins mentioned it." Sylvia Pool, a tall, elegantly dressed woman, interrupted. "Is it true you can really make a person act against his will?"

"No. However, a person can be conditioned to perform acts he would not otherwise do."

"Such as?" Sylvia asked, teasing. "What, for instance, could you condition me to do that I wouldn't ordinarily do?"

Ben laughed. "Well, there's the case of the Boston psychiatrist who used hypnosis to manipulate his patient sexually. The police arrested him two months ago. He used a trance to develop a dependent relationship with the woman. Then he introduced suggestions of erotic sexual fantasies. Gradually, through posthypnotic suggestions, he integrated himself into the woman's dreams, instilling in her a desire to act them out."

"Come on, Ben. That's not possible."

"With enough time and patience."

John grinned. "How long did it take this doctor?"

"Weekly sessions for about three months. He persuaded the woman to take an unsalaried job in his office and daily perform fellatio."

Sylvia blushed a deep shade of crimson.

"And this woman was in a trance the whole time?" John asked.

"Uh-uh. She was awake, acting out her dreams."

"It sure beats dry cleaning," Patrick exclaimed.

Amid laughter, Alison entered the room. "Dirty joke?"

"Dirty truth," Katherine answered. "Of course," she said to Ben, "testimony obtained under hypnosis is inadmissible in court."

"Testimony, yes, but evidence acquired under hypnosis has helped solved many crimes."

"Why is such testimony not allowed?"

Ben responded, "In a trance a person can so wish to please the hypnotist that he might lie."

"A hypnotized person is always supposed to tell the truth," Patrick said.

"Almost always. Most people do," Ben answered. "But as your wife will tell you, the extreme pressures on criminals and witnesses can influence what they say while under hypnosis."

Alison moved out of range of the conversation. She did not want to get involved in the subject of hypnosis. So far she'd been doing fine.

"Coffee will soon be ready," she said to Mrs. Blum. "Can I serve you anything?"

"No, thanks. I'm just enjoying being in this house again. I loved to visit Ruth. A wonderful woman. Very strong to have held up all those months. Never once broke down in public. In front of me it was different; we've been friends for years."

"Ben and I had very little chance to talk with her."

"You would have liked her husband, too. A professional piano player. When he scheduled recitals in Boston we always went. He specialized in the Romantics." She leaned toward Alison. "When I go, I hope it's fast. The lingering just preys on your mind."

"Yes," said Alison, thinking, God, what a depressing soul, then saying aloud, "I'd better circulate."

Nina had begun to clear the table, and Alison was bringing in the dessert when she felt a tug on her sleeve. It was Felicity Moritz, a graduate student. "Is there another bathroom? The line down here is a mile long."

"Upstairs," Alison said, putting down the cake she had baked that afternoon.

"Come with me. I'd like a tour."

"Felicity, roam around, everyone has."

"I can't just roam in someone else's house."

Nina shoved Alison. "Scat. I'll finish up here."

Felicity went into the bathroom off the master bedroom, and Alison waited for her in the bedroom in front of the full-length mirror. She appeared cool and composed, but the party was beginning to wear on her nerves. To fight her tiredness, she had drunk too much coffee. And surfacing, stronger than usual, was her eagerness for Friday's session. Alison began to grow fearful that in front of Ben and her guests she would lapse into one of those blank states.

"You look beautiful," Felicity said, emerging

from the bathroom. Alison showed off the walk-in closets, the dressing area, Ben's study, and the cupola in the hall.

"Another bathroom," Felicity said. "How extravagant. Alison, most women don't have a house until years after they're married. You have one while you're still living in sin."

"You're antediluvian, Felicity," Alison laughed. They continued down the hall.

"What's in here?" Felicity asked, turning the doorknob, but it would not give.

"Another bedroom, but it needs cleaning."

"That was Bruce's room." Mrs. Blum appeared beside them. "The bathroom downstairs is occupied."

"There's one—"

"Yes, I know. I've spent many hours up here."

"Can I see the room?" Felicity still held the knob.

"It's a mess."

"Must be," Mrs. Blum said. "After Bruce died, Ruth never went into that room again. Can't blame her, can you? Death lingers."

"What?" Felicity laughed. "Are you a medium or something?"

Oblivious to the question, Mrs. Blum added, "I lost my husband ten years ago, and his presence is still in the house." She disappeared into the bathroom.

"Poor guy," Felicity commented as she and Alison walked downstairs.

Noise from the living room rumbled up the stairs and engulfed Alison, and with it came the melodic notes from a piano. Alison covered her ears to block out the sound. At the foot of the steps she scolded herself. Keep busy. Talk. Entertain. Stan had arrived. He must have come while she was upstairs. Carol Mann was playing for the group surrounding the piano. Alison stifled the urge to ask Carol to stop playing. Curiously, the music was making her sleepy. Alison had to concentrate on something else quickly. She scanned the room for Ben, who was still talking with the Pools.

"I'm serious," he was saying to Sylvia, pulling Alison to him, an arm around her waist. "The frustration can be intolerable."

"Not that severe," retorted Sylvia.

"Worse. There's a case of a GP who was treating a woman for obesity, and, at his wit's end, he tried hypnosis. He hypnotized her and warned her that the next time she broke her diet she would kill her champion poodle. He figured the threat would act as a deterrent. Unfortunately, on the way home from his office she bought a gallon of ice cream, ate it, then killed her dog."

Ben and the Pools laughed loudly. The sound was painful to Alison. "That's not funny," she said, freeing herself from Ben and gazing, stone serious, at the Pools. She felt dizzy. "What Ben omitted is that the woman was so distraught over killing her dog she slashed her wrists." Louder laughter. Louder. Above the din, piano music filled her ears.

"Ali, what's the matter?" Ben asked.

Everyone's eyes were trained on her. Their stares oppressed her, driving her thoughts inward, the very direction she was fighting. In the ensuing silence she was more aware of the buzzing in her head, that static prelude to blacking out. Talk, she wanted to urge them. I need your conversation. But the burden of creating levity was hers. They waited expectantly. Her mind clouded. Sne could barely construct a simple sentence much less a scintillating one that would shatter the awkward silence. She said feebly, "I'm sorry, I've had too much wine." She was drifting and couldn't snap out of it.

"I'll get some coffee," Nina said.

"I have Compozine if you're feeling queasy," Katherine offered. Someone advised baking soda, someone else suggested Alka-Seltzer. Another voice recommended sleep. Alison moved toward Ben, stumbled, and Stan caught her. A chill rushed up her spine, fanning out across her neck and shoulders to her arms, numbing her body. If only Ben would hold the session now, she thought wildly. Now! Not Friday. She'd give anything for a respite from these spells. She struggled against losing consciousness and pretended to be drunk.

"Ali, I'm surprised at you," Ben joked.

"This must be a first," Felicity chimed in. "The girl who barely imbibes is four sheets to the wind."

They japed with the humor that the mildly intoxicated reserve for the drunken as Ben guided her upstairs. Nina tucked in the blanket, asking if Alison felt nauseated. "She should take the Compozine."

"Actually," Ben said, "she'll be better off getting sick to her stomach if she's overdone it." He sat beside her holding her hand, and she fell asleep immediately.

# 14

By Friday Ben couldn't remember when he had been saddled with so many problems. He was anxious about Alison, who seemed tense and overwrought since they'd moved, and it bothered him that she was falling behind in her studies. He was also very worried about the next session and was grateful that Pollack would be there to lend him moral support. He'd been so preoccupied that he'd forgotten to tell Stan that Pollack would be present. But Stan didn't mind.

Ben hid his nervousness as he added a chair to the triangle, making a diamond configuration. On his way to the office he'd bumped into Hopkins, who said that Ben's latest progress report was still too skimpy, that his evaluations and conclusions needed elaboration. Ben hoped that after this session he would be able to deliver some meaningful facts—and interpretations.

Alison, Stan, and Pollack sat in their chairs. Ben joined them, sitting opposite Pollack. "This time, Ali, you begin the volleying."

"You don't like my serve?" Stan asked.

"Just manipulation of protocol. Nothing personal."

Alison shifted to a more comfortable position, her hands in her lap, looking down at Stan's legs. "Close your eyes and rest your hands on your thighs, palms open."

Eyes closed, Stan took long, deep breaths. Before Alison had even uttered the first words of induction, he'd slipped into a light trance.

She mentioned Stan's growing awareness of the texture of his pants, the warmth of his hands on his legs. It was a different technique: focusing on tactile sensations. Her face showed her amazement as she registered the speed with which Stan's trance deepened. It occurred to Ben that he should have prepared her for this. To see if happen suddenly might frighten her, but she continued calmly.

One minute. Stan's posture drooped, his head hung supported by a rubbery neck. Occasionally Alison glanced at Ben, but she never disrupted her induction. Pollack crossed his legs, his gaze fixed on Stan. A yellow pad balanced precariously on his knees, ready to fall.

"You feel as though a helium-filled balloon were tied to your wrist, gently tugging your arm upward."

The effect was immediate. Stan's wrist arched, his fingers hung loose, barely grazing his pants. Lifted magically by Alison's words, his arm ascended with the liquid motion of a dancer. Alison laced the ascent with suggestions of drowsiness and sleep. Ben reached for the camera, which he now kept close by, momentarily interrupting Alison's concentration. From across the room he shot two photographs. Stan appeared life-less, his wrist strung up by an invisible cord. Ben took a closeup, then checked his stopwatch and held up a finger to Alison, indicating that one minute remained. She had Stan lower his arm gradually, suggesting that he fall into a deeper trance with the descending motion. When the induction was over, Ben noticed Alison rubbing her hands together.

"Honey, are you cold?" Ben asked.

"Freezing."

He switched on the electric heater and draped a sweater around her shoulders. She was shivering.

"Do you feel ill?"

"No, I'm all right."

"The room will be warmer in a few minutes. Would you get a reading from Stan?"

The depth of only thirty-five surprised Ben, and he had Alison repeat the question. Stan said thirty-five again. Alison instructed Stan to hypnotize her, and as she did, Ben whispered in her ear. She added, "Dr. West will tell you when to stop. You must obey his instructions."

Stan told Alison to concentrate on her breathing. After only a few seconds, her eyes closed. Each breath lulled her into a more restful state, softening the muscles of her face. Stan had her visualize a blue vapor flaring from her nose, feel it brush her lips. When five minutes had passed, Ben squeezed Stan's shoulder. "This is Dr. West." Be precise. Speak loudly. Allow no chance for misunderstanding, Ben reminded himself. Yet he found himself torn between hoping the session would run smoothly and wanting something dramatic to happen for Pollack's sake. "You hear my voice clearly. You hear each word perfectly. I order you to stop hypnotizing Alison."

Stan fell silent. There was no change in his expression or in the tone of his voice. Ben ordered Stan to elicit Alison's depth.

"Forty-one." Her voice was clear.

"They've gone much deeper than this," Ben said to Pollack.

"You've changed the setup," Pollack reminded him. "It would be unlikely that the pattern remained the same." He quipped, "What a pity. Only a deep trance after five grueling minutes of induction."

Placing his hand on Alison's shoulder, Ben said, "This is Dr. West. You hear my voice clearly. You hear each word perfectly. I order you to deepen Stan's trance."

Alison conjured the image of a leaf falling in slow motion, oscillating to and fro as it edged its way toward the ground. Ben was puzzled. What was the rationale for the techniques they were using? Certainly there was no consistency here. Twice during the five minutes he leaned Stan back against his chair. When Ben instructed Alison to stop hypnotizing Stan she obeyed. Ben looked at Pollack, who was taking notes.

"Everything seems normal," whispered Pollack.

"Your explicit statements leave no room for confusion." He held up his pad, on which he'd written: "Let's hear their voices again." He did not want his request to suggest to Alison and Stan that their voices were under examination.

Ben was about to ask Stan for a depth reading when he observed a sudden drop in his respiration rate. He counted eight breaths a minute. Pollack took Stan's pulse. "Thirty-two."

"What is your trance depth?" Ben asked, concerned.

"Twooo huundreeed...twooooo huuuundreeeeed...twooooo huuundreeeeeeed..." The echo was faint and hair-thin but had the cutting edge of a sharp steel knife. It sent a chill through Ben. He was eager for the reverberations to fade.

Pollack shook his head. "Incredible! Stan is locked into some body clock."

With a hand on Alison's shoulder, Ben asked, "How do you feel?"

"Happy. Very content. I wish I could always feel this way." Her voice sounded weak and hollow and had the familiar mechanical tone, but there was no echo.

"The deeper they go, the more distant they feel from wakeful reality orientation," Pollack said. "That's a natural result of a trance. But for some unexplained reason, their awareness of distance manifests itself in their voices. Maybe their mutual trance is far more real to them than a conventional one. Perhaps, to enhance the cave's reality, they unconsciously alter their voices to sound like natural cave echoes. But that's a wild guess."

Ben touched Stan's shoulder. "This is Dr. West.

You hear my voice clearly. You hear every word perfectly. I order you to deepen Alison's trance. I will tell you when to stop. And you will."

"We are at the entrance of a long cave. We are walking inside. You can see the drawings on the walls of the cave. We have been here before."

How in the world did Stan remember, was the first question that struck Ben. *We have been here before.* There was no equivocation in his words. Despite the posthypnotic suggestion to forget everything during the sessions, Stan remembered. And as before, Stan did not suggest that the excursion into the cave would deepen Alison's trance, yet that's exactly the effect it had. Ben had never seen a subject's face so expressionless. Alison's features seemed to merge, wash out.

Pollack pointed to Stan. He, too, had immediately grasped the improbability of what was happening. The rock formations Stan described, the brilliant light, seemed a verbatim replay of the previous session. The only variation was in Stan's voice, which sounded richer, more animated than before.

"You hear music coming from up ahead. It will grow louder as we proceed."

Ben flashed back to Stan's defiant expression from the last session. Then he experienced a new vague fear, one he could not identify.

Alison fell forward. Ben and Pollack grabbed her at the same time. She could no longer sit upright in her chair. Ben went to the closet for a cot. He unfolded it next to her chair, and he and Pollack lifed her onto it. She was dead weight. Stan's voice ran on. He showed no awareness of Alison's

100

reaction. The brilliant light became an obsession with him, its color a golden yellow that changed to white as he and Alison approached it. It was the source of the music, if Ben understood correctly. The light *was* the music. Stan equated the two, attributing warmth to the music and rhythm to the light. The light lulled, and the music shone. Several times Stan instructed Alison to listen to the light.

Two and a half minutes remained. Alison's breathing was extremely slow. Ben began to count and signaled Pollack to measure her pulse rate.

"Take a deep breath," Stan said. Alison's chest expanded. "Smell the flowers. Gardenias."

Ingenious, Ben thought. Stan had engaged another sense. First vision, then hearing and touch, now smell. Four of the five senses, all to increase the reality of the cave. Suddenly Ben tensed as it dawned on him that Stan had specified gardenias. Alison's favorite flower. She was taking only four breaths a minute, but the expansion of her chest increased as she inhaled the fragrance of the flowers. Pollack held up his pad for Ben: fifteen beats a minute. Less than a quarter of a normal rate. She was going into a state of suspended animation, a state generally achieved only in the deepest meditation.

"There's no cause for alarm," Pollack said, catching the anxious expression on Ben's face. "The body's metabolism can safely function at far slower paces." That's true, Ben reassured himself. It did with certain drugs and in hypothermia, when a patient's body is frozen during surgery to reduce bleeding and shock. Physiology can slow to a crawl but does not stop of its own accord. And never in a trance. The instinct for self-preservation is innate and automatic. True. But it made no difference. Ben could not control his panic. He had to end the session.

Ben rested his hand on Stan's shoulder. "This is Dr. West. You can hear my voice clearly." Ben hoped that neither Stan nor Pollack noticed the quaver in his voice. "You can hear each word perfectly. I order you to stop hypnotizing Alison."

"Hear the light. It grows—"

"Louder," Pollack said.

Ben raised his voice. "In compliance with your posthypnotic suggestion, you cannot disobey. I order you to stop at once."

Stan was silent.

Ben slumped in his chair, drained. There had been no trace of defiance in Stan's face. Merely a moment's delay. He expected a sapient "I told you so" from Pollack, but he didn't care. Stan had obeyed, and that was all that mattered to Ben. He wiped the perspiration from his face.

Pollack leaned over the cot, studying Alison. "Her trance is profound." He touched her cheek and ran his fingers from her jaw to her eye. "Feel her."

"She's ice cold. Her skin has no texture." Or was it that he was so shaken that *he* was numb? Her lips were drawn back at the corners. Ben lifted her eyelids. Her eyes had rolled back in her head.

"I've never witnessed anything like it!" Pollack declared.

"I'm going to awaken her," Ben said.

"Without a depth? You're crazy!"

Ben stared at Alison.

"Control yourself, Ben. Your emotions are fogging your reason."

"I'm terminating this session." He reached for Alison's shoulder, but Pollack grabbed his hand.

"First, get her depth. I've never seen such a profound state. Don't be a fool."

As Ben put his hand on Alison's shoulder, Pollack picked up the camera and shot a picture from above the cot.

"This is Dr. West. You hear me clearly. What is your depth?"

Her lips barely moved, and an echo filled the room. "Nooo deeepth . . . nooo deeeepth . . . noooooodeeeeepth . . . nooooooodeeeeepth . . ."

The sound stung his ears, and its duration was mercifully brief, for Alison's energy level was very low. Ben stared blankly at her.

"It only means that she'd unable to make an estimate," Pollack interjected quickly. "It's miraculous that subjects are able to extrapolate the scale in the first place. You can't go into shock simply because she's lost the ability to judge her depth."

Ben felt Alison's face. The tape recorder accumulated a long stretch of silence before Pollack spoke. "The cave must be extraordinarily real. Test her."

Ben glared at him.

"Test her. Ask her to pick a flower and bring it back to the office when she awakens."

"Damn it, I'm terminating this session," Ben shouted.

"Not until you investigate Alison's trance. This could be a big breakthrough, so don't blow it. You could be on the verge of an important discovery. There's something here just waiting to be uncovered. Besides, you're afraid of Stan's reactions, not Alison's."

Pollack was right. Even Alison's depth did not trouble him as much as the dread that he might lose control over Stan.

Pollack urged, "Leave Stan out of this, but for God's sake, don't awaken Alison before testing her trance."

It was not Pollack's prodding but Ben's own instinct, framed by vague suspicions, that finally convinced him to continue. Leaning over the cot and touching her shoulder, he said, "This is Dr. West. Alison, where are the gardenias?"

*"They are in front of me."* Ben flinched at the echo.

"I want you to select one flower and pick it. On awakening you will bring it back to my office. I would like to smell it."

Her right arm rose. Ben had been curious whether she would make a physical gesture or merely comply mentally. She searched the air, her hand open, fingers spread apart. Her motion was circular, methodical, as though there were so many flowers to choose from she couldn't decide which to pick.

"Stan!" Pollack whispered. Ben wheeled around. Stan's blank expression had been replaced by one of anger, his lips pressed into a taut line.

Alison's hand fell back to the cot.

"Again," Pollack said.

"I order you to pick a flower."

Hesitantly, her hand lifted. But this time it was closed in a fist. She groped awkwardly, as if about to pluck a flower, then withdrew her hand quickly, as if she'd encountered a hot surface.

Ben tightened his grip. "I order you to pick the flower directly in front of you."

Her forehead wrinkled in confusion and conster-
nation, revealing signs of an internal struggle. Her
hand opened, then closed.

Pollack photographed Stan. The expression on
Stan's face sickened Ben. Utter defiance frozen in
place. Contempt carved in granite. Ben flushed with
anger as he gripped Alison's shoulder.

"I ORDER YOU TO PICK A FLOWER!" The
camera flashed, blinding him for a second.

The frustration in Alison's face upset him. She
seemed near tears. Her arm jerked back and forth as
though invisible ropes tugged at it.

"Again." Pollack raised his voice. "Stan's deliberately defying you."

Ben's heart was pounding. He'd had enough. He
wanted to relieve Alison of her terrible anguish, but
he couldn't just yet. His knowledge that he had to
force *his* control over the session and a growing fear
drove him on.

"Give the order again." Pollack was almost
yelling as he aimed the camera at Stan.

Alison squirmed on the cot.

"I ORDER YOU TO PICK A FLOWER."

Her arm lurched forward, slapping Ben in the
face. Her whole body trembled.

"ALISON, YOU MUST LISTEN TO ME!"

Sweat broke out on her forehead.

"Be firmer. *You* must dominate."

"YOU DO HEAR MY VOICE. YOU MUST
OBEY. I ORDER YOU TO PICK A GARDE-
NIA."

Alison's eyes opened. Ben's hand was digging
into her shoulder. She appeared groggy, stunned, as
she focused on Ben, then Pollack, then scanned the
room. She tried to sit up but was sapped of energy,

so Ben helped her. She looked haggard. Perspiration rolled down her face. Her legs hung limply over the side of the cot. Ben realized that his shirt was soaking wet.

She studied the cot, then looked over at Stan. Ben followed her gaze. Stan's face was expressionless. He sat erect. A tic had developed in his right eye.

Alison leaned against Ben.

"Dizzy, honey?"

"Tired. And thirsty. I'd like some water." She gestured at the cot and smiled wanly. "I must have gotten pretty sloppy."

"Alison," Pollack asked, "do you remember anything? Anything at all?"

She faced Ben. "Is something wrong? What happened?"

"No, Ali, everything's fine."

But she did not feel fine. This was the first time she'd awakened from a session exhausted and nauseated. Ben's smile and convivial manner cautioned her from asking further questions. Thank God there was only the weekend to navigate before confiding everything to Dr. Goodman. "Do you want me to awaken Stan?" she asked.

"No, honey, you take it easy." At Ben's command, Stan awakened without incident, apparently oblivious to his trance behavior.

Around eight-thirty that evening, Pollack phoned to check on Alison. He and Ben had not been able to discuss anything in her presence following the session. "She's quiet. Otherwise she appears to be okay," Ben said in a hushed voice that would be inaudible to Alison in the kitchen. "But I'm not going to leave her alone."

"Something bizarre is happening that Ali and Stan are probably unaware of themselves. I've been thinking that the only way to solve this riddle is for you to hypnotize Alison alone and interrogate her. Somewhere deep in her subconscious are answers."

Keeping the call brief so as not to arouse Alison's suspicions, Ben thanked Pollack for his concern and vowed to hypnotize Alison at the first chance he had. Returning to the kitchen, he realized how apprehensive he had already become at the thought of what she might reveal in a trance.

# 15

"It's a novel concept," Dr. Goodman commented, lighting his pipe. His tan accentuated his natural buoyancy, a sharp contrast to Alison's mood. "How long have you been involved in this?"

"About two months—we missed only one week. Could the therapy really cause the blackouts?" He sighted down an invisible line that skimmed the top of her head and extended to some mysterious point on the bookshelf behind her—where he always looked after she asked a question.

"Would you prefer to drop out of these sessions, Alison?"

"Only if they're causing the problem. Otherwise,

no. I'm not having nightmares as frequently, and that's a luxury for me. And the hypnosis also gives me a few peaceful hours that I need." Dr. Goodman was deep in thought. She had struggled to explain everything coherently, organizing all the details in sequence—at least all that she remembered. It was a comfort being with him.

"Alison, since I'm no longer your therapist, I can't in good conscience advise you on any decisions. However, I am concerned about your blackouts. Why haven't you told Ben about your symptoms?"

"Ben is using his sessions with me as a pilot study for a grant to investigate mutual hypnosis. I wouldn't want him to think my blackouts are related to his therapy unless they really are."

"Do you think the two affect each other?"

After a moment of silence, she answered, "At first I was certain they did. But now I feel the blackouts are an evolution of my neurosis."

Dr. Goodman smiled. "Why do you believe that?"

She squeezed her hands together. "Twice last week I sat down to write my father, and each time I dissociated and awoke not knowing how much time had passed."

Dr. Goodman nodded. "Well, a hypnotic trance is harmless per se. Still, your blacking out bothers me."

So, she thought, he did not think they were related to the sessions. That was a great relief.

"Alison, remember telling me about your reaction as a child when your father created embarassing scenes?"

"Yes, I defocused so I couldn't see him—or Mother, or anything. It was an escape."

"Not much different perhaps from what you're doing now."

"So I *am* causing the blackouts." Then her fear that she was sick had been justified. "What brings on dissociation?"

"Many things. Inability to cope with a painful situation. Trauma. Severe guilt feelings." He glanced at her lap; she was wringing her hands. "Have I struck a nerve?"

Alison explained to him her reluctance to invite her father to the wedding. That she'd written the note only after Ben had nagged her about it, but she couldn't bring herself to sign or mail it.

"Do you want your father at the wedding?"

"No." Her answer shocked her. She had told Ben—and believed it herself—that she was reconciled to her father's presence at the wedding. Apparently that had been a grand self-deception. She and Dr. Goodman discussed her father briefly since he was already well acquainted with her feelings. Then their conversation swung around to her relationship with Ben. She admitted that the fevers, headaches, and nausea had of course interfered with their sex life and that her sexual desire was at a low ebb. Lately, Ben had been pressuring her into making love. And he was argumentative and irritable, uncharacteristic traits that frightened her.

"He's been possessive recently," she added. "He insists that we spend more time together. It's because he's worried about me—and his work. I have a hunch he's disturbed about the sessions though he won't discuss it with Stan or me. Dean Hopkins turned him down for a grant, which was something of a disappointment, but there's a chance Hopkins will award the grant further along in the project."

"What makes you think Ben's upset about the sessions?"

"Last Friday he had an observer, Dr. Pollack, sit in. He's never done that before. I think he's hoping that Pollack can help him with whatever the problem is. Anyway, for various reasons, we're both under a lot of strain these days."

"It goes without saying that you enjoy Ben's company."

"Of course, and I don't mind his possessiveness." She did mind, but she didn't fight it because she was growing afraid to be alone. She accepted his following her around, watching her so closely that she almost felt like a burglar in her own house. Alison crossed her legs and wiped her damp palms on her dress.

"Is there something else you want to tell me?"

She hedged for a moment. "I look forward to the sessions. Even when I began to suspect they might be screwing me up, I didn't want them to end. Is that masochistic?"

Goodman laughed, and his enormous belly bounced above the desk. "You used to say that our visits were the highlights of your week."

She had forgotten that. Forgotten how she had checked off on the calendar days between appointments, how she'd made notes, and how before each meeting she rehearsed the things she intended to discuss with him.

"Alison, I have patients who would see me every day if they could afford it—or if I'd let them." He wrote on his pad, then pointed his pen at her. "I don't like the blackouts and advise you to resume therapy with me—it won't interfere with Ben's experiment. In fact, I'll broach this to Ben, if you'd like."

"Oh, no. Please don't. I'm sure Ben would regard my seeing you even this once as a failure on his part. Let me find the right way—and time—to tell him."

"Okay, I understand, but I want you to do it soon, if possible." He handed her a prescription. "This will relieve anxiety. And it should keep those headaches from returning."

Ben arrived home at five o'clock. From the foyer he shouted for Alison, but she didn't respond. Where the hell was she? he wondered. He heard a noise upstairs and followed it.

"Ali?" he called louder.

He was furious and sick with worry. She had not shown up for lunch again, no one could locate her at the university, and between classes he had repeatedly phoned but had got no answer. Standing in the doorway of the master bedroom, he scolded her. "Didn't you hear me downstairs? This is why you missed more classes?" Alison stood on the stepladder, painting the ceiling. "I must have phoned four or five times. Did you know Bronson scheduled a test for today?"

"No," she answered softly.

"Why didn't you answer the phone?"

"I figured it might be Nina, and I wasn't in the mood to gossip."

Only then did Ben notice her pants, and his voice jumped an octave. "Why haven't you returned those pants?"

"They're old. Stan said I could keep them for painting."

Ben threw his briefcase onto the bed. "Come down from there right now and take them off."

"Why?" she asked, startled, as she climbed down.

"They're hardly flattering, that's why."

"Ben, I don't wear them in public. I'm—"

"I don't care. I don't want you wearing them."

She had never seen him that angry. Quickly she slipped into a pair of dungarees, avoiding his eyes. He tossed Stan's pants into his study.

"What have I done that's so terrible?" she asked, fighting back tears. It was his turn to look away. "You've been so sharp with me lately. Tell me what's wrong so I can apologize." She began to cry.

Ben's anger disappeared, and he held her in his arms. "Honey, it's me, not you. I'm sorry." This was the first time he'd made her cry, and that realization nearly brought tears to his eyes. He rocked her in his arms until she stopped sobbing, then, before he quite knew what he was doing, he backed her to the bed and began undressing her. When she attempted to help, he brushed her hands aside. His movements became more forceful, alarming her. He undressed with the same urgency, and in bed his usual gentleness was replaced with a frenzy, an obsessive desire to dominate her. She submitted, not sure whether she was trying to please him or was afraid to resist.

While she prepared dinner, he finished painting the ceiling. As they ate in a strained silence, she knew she could not possibly mention her visit to Dr. Goodman. It might set him off again. She tried to start a conversation by talking about the wedding, though now was not the time to spring the idea of a church service on him. She brought up the wedding reception, but didn't pursue it when he was slow to respond.

While Alison cleared the table, Ben went to the phone in the hall. Pollack had sailed into him that afternoon for not carrying out his promise to hypnotize and question Alison. Embarrassed to express his increasing apprehension about what she might reveal, he argued that first he wanted to search the tape for clues—and particularly to compare the wording of the cave sequences from the last two sessions. He had asked Mrs. DiVetto to finish the transcriptions as quickly as possible. He had dialed three digits of her number when he noticed a scrap of paper next to the telephone directory. It was a message that Mrs. DiVetto had called to say her work had been delayed. The message was scribbled and hard to read, unlike Alison's precise handwriting. He was irritated both with Mrs. DiVetto for phoning the house when he had emphatically instructed her to call him only at the office and with Alison for forgetting to give him the message. He laid the note on the kitchen table.

Alison placed a bowl of stewed fruit beside him, then poured coffee.

"When did Mrs. DiVetto call?"

"Oh, I'm sorry. I forgot to tell you. This afternoon."

"What time?"

"About one-thirty or two."

"Who took the message?"

She was puzzled. "I did."

"Ali, you didn't pick up the phone today."

"Not once I started painting." He was making her feel like a criminal again, but she couldn't reveal that she'd been out of the house, at Dr. Goodman's office. She scooped fruit into a bowl and put it in front of him.

"Did Mrs. DiVetto explain why she called me here?"

"She said she tried to reach you at the office, but your line was busy. What did she want?"

"Was everything on the tape discernible?"

"Ben, how should I know?" The throbbing in her head began again. Relax, she warned herself, it's anxiety. She excused herself, went upstairs, and took a pill from Dr. Goodman's prescription. She'd hidden the bottle in her closet. She was about to swallow the capsule when her stomach started spasming. She bent over the toilet and threw up her dinner. Afterward she washed her face, brushed her teeth, and washed down another pill with water. She studied her face in the mirror. It was calm, practically emotionless, but that wasn't how she felt. She returned to the kitchen, her headache nearly unbearable.

"I was beginning to wonder what was keeping you. Your coffee's cold. Did Mrs. DiVetto mention when she might be finished?"

"A day. Two. I don't recall." Her head hurt even more when she talked.

"She must have given an explanation for the delay."

Alison whispered, "The quality of the tape was poor."

"Ali, why didn't you tell me?"

"I forgot," She had no more patience for his attacks on her.

"Is there anything else you forgot?"

Her head was about to split open. "No!" she shouted. "Leave me alone. What do you want from me?"

The outburst caught him off guard. In the ensuing silence it occurred to him how unmercifully he'd been questioning her, and he felt contrite.

"Ali, I didn't mean to—"

"Shut up!" The pain exploded in her head; every word she spoke was a knife jabbing at her temples.

"Ali," he stammered, dumbstruck. "Honey?"

"Leave me alone! Don't you understand?"

As he stood up, she ran from the table. Speechless, he followed her to the living room, where she slumped onto the sofa, her head in her hands. He sat down beside her. Then he remembered, next week to the day marked a year since her mother's death. No wonder she was so upset, and it was callous of him to have let it slip his mind. "Honey, please forgive me." She did not acknowledge his presence. "I've been awful these past few days, a real prick. But things will be different, I swear. I've been bringing my work home with me, so to speak, and as you know, I've been worried about you."

Alison looked at him. The medication was taking effect, so the pain was tolerable. Ben continued to apologize, kissing and fondling her, and his voice and touch were easier to bear. But she was glad when he left her alone to do the dishes.

When he returned, Alison was fast asleep. He sat in the chair near the sofa and read, periodically glancing at her. He finished reading close to midnight and gently shook her awake. "Don't get up." Lifting her in his arms, he carried her upstairs. This aroused him, and again he experienced an irresistible need to possess her.

The air in their bedroom smelled oily with paint. He realized he should have ventilated the room while they were downstairs. He settled Alison on the bed in the guest room, ignoring her weak protests while he undressed her.

Alison dreamed she was at the beach. The sun warmed her back and melted away her embarrassment. Her father had been intentionally rude to her and her friends. It was not an accident; he had deliberately ruined her birthday party. Her friends would gossip about it tomorrow at school.

She spread her towel in the dunes where the tall reeds and beach grass formed a natural shelter from the wind. He had promised to behave, but had disappointed her yet again. The air smelled salty. She ran her tongue over her upper lip, then licked her arm. Her entire body was covered with a layer of invisible crystals. She couldn't see them but could taste them.

Gulls strutted in the sand. Thousands of them. They aligned themselves into a perfect square, a pageant staged for her tenth birthday. When the last gull joined the square, the flock took wing, flying in a square formation.

The sky darkened and it began to rain. Suddenly there was thunder and lightning. One bolt hit the birds, transforming them into black crows. They flew in a circular pattern, spiraling toward her. Diving faster and faster. She ran, but the heavy sheets of rain weighed her down. The birds made raspy, raucous sounds, calling, "Alison! Alison! Alison!" One of the crows struck her neck, puncturing her skin. Another swooped by her, driving its iron beak into her back. The wind forced her screams back. She couldn't breathe. They pecked at her face and tongue, pierced her eyes. Her face was sticky with blood. She buried her face in the sand, gasping for air. Air. Air.

It was over. He had had that nightmare again. That horrible dream about Alison. The room was cold; the sheets wet with perspiration. The iridescent clock read three-thirty. Shivering, Stan pulled up the covers, turned away from Nina and tried to fall back to sleep.

# 16

"What time is it?" Ben said sleepily.

"Six, buddy," Pollack replied. "Sorry to rouse you so early, but you weren't around last night, and I'm leaving for Vermont in a few hours."

Ben rubbed his eyes and managed to sit up. "My first Wednesday class isn't until nine."

"I'm holding the transcripts in my hot little hands," Pollack said. "You ought to read them. Shall I stop by?"

"No." Ben lowered his voice. "Alison's asleep." She was lying on her side, her arms wrapped around her pillow. She had kicked off the covers, and with his free hand Ben pulled them over her. "I'll be at your place in about twenty minutes."

He dressed quietly.

Monday night's nightmare had left Alison so terribly shaken that Ben wondered if Mrs. DiVetto had told her something that could have added to her hysteria. He had again questioned Alison, but she insisted that it was just the nightmare that had upset her.

On Tuesday morning Ben had phoned Mrs. DiVetto. Yes, she had spoken to Alison. No, she had revealed nothing except the poor quality of the tape. The hum was still there, stronger and more frequent, drowning out words. With luck she might finish transcribing it that night. She promised to contact him the minute she was through.

"Dr. West," she said as they concluded the conversation, "I won't be able to work on the tapes anymore." Her excuse was that they took far too much time away from her family. Ben could not change her mind. The persistent hum puzzled him, and he made a note to check his tape recorder for mechanical malfunction.

On Tuesday evening Alison had surprised him with two tickets for an Alicia de Larrocha concert in Boston. She had bought them more than a month before and was in such good spirits that Ben was able to hide his annoyance. He called Pollack immediately to see if he'd be in and arranged for Mrs. DiVetto to phone him. They did not get home until after midnight, a long evening for Ben, who fidgeted throughout the concert. As soon as he walked in the door he called Pollack, who either wasn't home or wasn't answering his phone.

Ben laid a note on his pillow: "Couldn't sleep. Went to the office early. See you for lunch. Love."

• • •

Pollack's two-room apartment, three miles from campus, might as well have been inhabited by a fraternity. The kitchenette was littered with dirty dishes and glasses. Garish Indian fabric draped the sofa and two chairs, and pillows covered with cat fur were strewn over the floor. Nestled on one cluster of pillows were three beige Himalayans.

"Where were you last night? I called after midnight."

"I was out carousing and celebrating an exciting discovery. But let's start at the beginning. Sit down." He handed the transcripts to Ben. "The cave sequences are the same." Ben compared them for himself. Word for word. The transcripts were identical—and that was a phenomenon!

"Amazing." Ben shook his head. "That's worth celebrating."

"My discovery is still to come, buddy. You've overlooked something."

Ben reread the transcripts. Chunks of dialogue were missing, the lacunae filled with series of dots. "That damn hum has obliterated some important stuff."

"Don't feel badly." Pollack was gloating. "I missed it on the first reading myself. Here." He flipped through the pages in Ben's hands. "It was only after a few joints that I spotted it. Start with this line."

The cave sequence. Ben carefully perused it twice. "Sorry. Whatever it is, I'm missing it."

Pollack took the manuscript from Ben and read aloud: "We are standing at the entrance of a cave.

We are going inside. When we see the light we will know we are heading in the right direction."

Ben nodded innocently. "It's too early in the day for me."

Pollack skipped ahead, reading random sentences. "The light comes from the end of the cave. We can see it from here. We must approach it gradually."

"All right, so I'm dense." Ben was tired of Pollack's pomposity.

*"We!"* Pollack announced emphatically, *"we.* Stan used the plural during both inductions!"

A knot formed in Ben's chest. "A hypnotist often uses the plural." He shrugged. "It lends credibility to the fantasy. It increases rapport with the subject."

"The conventional hypnotist is *awake* when he includes himself in his subject's fantasy," Pollack said. "However, the hypnotist is well aware that he is *not* part of the adventure. Stan, buddy, was hypnotized. He was an integral part of the fantasy he created."

"Stan..." Ben's voice died away.

"Yes, Stan deepened his own trance at the same time he deepened Alison's trance. He accompanied her into the cave. In the last session, you awakened Stan without recording his depth."

"He was in a light trance," Ben snapped. The knot tightened within him.

"Exactly. But he'd been in a stupor just moments before."

The bedroom door opened, and a woman wearing one of Pollack's shirts paraded into the room.

"Patti, meet Ben West."

"Hi, Ben."

"Hello."

She plopped herself onto the pillow in front of them, crossing her legs. As an afterthought, she yanked the shirttail between them. "There's a serious powwow going on out here. What's doing?"

"Ben and I are having a stag party. You be a love and rustle up some breakfast."

Ben held up his hand. "Not for me, please. I'll have breakfast when I get home." He was ready to leave.

"That's cool," Patti said, scooting into the kitchen. Ben hoped she would not overhear their conversation.

"How long will you be in Vermont?"

"Two days." Pollack nodded toward the bedroom and grinned. "We *all* have Friday classes."

"We'll finish this discussion then."

"Hold it. I'm not through yet. Have you hypnotized Alison?"

"Not yet."

"The only way to find out what's happening between Alison and Stan during the sessions is to hypnotize Alison and interrogate her."

"Alison hasn't been feeling well lately."

"That's no excuse."

"It's excuse enough for me." Was Ben more upset at Pollack's flippant attitude or at the implications of his discovery? Whichever, the knot in his chest was a rock-hard lump of jealousy.

"You should question her before the next session. I would—"

"There won't be another session."

"Come on, buddy, you're acting silly. It's vital that they continue. Especially now."

"There'll be no more sessions."

Pollack's frown relaxed into a condescending smile. "Certainly you're not afraid that you'll be unable to awaken them?"

"No, I'm not." His fear was of an entirely different nature.

"Good, because no subject has ever been locked into a trance. That shit's just layman's lore. Even if you abandon a subject in a *plenary* trance, he'll eventually fall into a natural sleep and awaken." He laughed. "I once did that, unintentionally, of course. I dozed off while a subject was in a trance, and when I awoke, she was fast asleep in my bed."

"Who was she?" Patti returned with a tray.

"Love, you don't know her."

Ben collected the transcripts and put on his coat.

"Whoa, where are you going?" Pollack said, following Ben.

Ben opened the door.

"Hold on, Ben. I'm not trying to take over your experiment, but you did seek my help, if you recall. I'm only explaining to you what's going on and what you can do about it. At least hear me out."

Ben started down the corridor, mad with jealousy.

Pollack stood in the doorway. "You're tampering with stuff hotter than you think," he shouted. "Okay, suit yourself. But you'll be back. You'll sure as hell be back."

# 17

Alison read the note Ben had left her. She had overslept. It was already two o'clock. She'd missed her three classes, and she didn't care. Since Monday she'd been too confused to think about much but the hallucination she'd had. It wasn't a dream. It seemed different somehow from a dream. Was it a side effect of the drug? She stood at the window, trying to recall the hallucination. Ice flowers coated the pane. She scratched abstract designs on the glass with her finger, then dug the ice from beneath her nail.

She washed, combed her hair, and put on a jersey top and wool slacks. She decided to take the medication only if her headache got worse. For the time being the pain was bearable. She called Goodman to check if the painkiller or whatever he'd prescribed could cause hallucinations, but his service answered that he was busy with a patient. A faint memory of the hallucination was crystallizing in her mind. Blackbirds. Yes, blackbirds had appeared in so many of her dreams, but she was sure this wasn't a dream. This was different, more real and more strange. She flashed on floating and meaningless words, a foreign language maybe, ringing in her ears. She was lying across a bed shrouded by a white mist. She had no boundaries, no weight, no substance. A body hovered just above her. She couldn't move closer to it to see if she could recognize whoever it was because she felt paralyzed. Her body didn't respond. She had no control over her it, nor did she seem to want any. Throughout the night she'd slept with that body hovering above her.

The sensation she'd had was similar to her experiences as a sophomore at Wesleyan when she'd volunteered to participate in an experimental drug study. She was never informed which hallucinogens were used, but this feeling of externally observing herself or being observed was somewhat familiar. If the hallucination was not a result of the drug Goodman had prescribed, did that mean her illness caused it? She wondered. And if her illness caused it, did that mean she was getting worse?

Alison shook her head. She couldn't consider this alternative. Hoping to clear her mind, she puttered around in the guest room, concentrating on cleaning it up. She watered and misted the gardenia plant, whose two blossoms sweetly scented the air. Then she went downstairs and made herself coffee and toast, which she took to the living room since it was warmer than the kitchen. Her headache had lessened. The melody of one of de Larrocha's pieces popped into her head. Alison gave in to the temptation and sat at the piano. With one finger she began striking the keys. The right-hand part came easily, a simple melody: B,D,E,F sharp, G,A,B,C,E,E. That was the motif. She continued piecing it together. It didn't take her long to figure out the left-hand part, sequences of arpeggios, but her fingers tripped clumsily over each other.

She sat up with a start, wondering how long the doorbell had been ringing. It was her first blackout since seeing Dr. Goodman.

"I took a chance that you might be home." Nina dropped her coat on the living room couch. "Alison, I hope I'm not bothering you, but I must talk to someone."

"You've been crying," Alison observed, her tone callously unconcerned.

"Stan moved out. Last night. I phoned the dormitory where he's staying, but he won't speak to me. Ali, I haven't the slightest idea what caused this. He simply walked out."

"Was it your fault?"

"No, it wasn't. He's been so moody lately—I can't judge when a remark will make him laugh or throw a tantrum—but this time we hadn't even been quarreling."

"Would you like coffee?"

"Ali, you don't understand. This isn't just another one of our fights. It's serious."

"He wants a divorce?"

"Well, yes. Yes, he does." Nina paused. "Has Stan already mentioned this to you or Ben?"

"No." Alison went to the kitchen and returned with two cups of coffee.

"The last time he walked out on me," Nina continued, "was when he had that affair with that freshman." She sipped her coffee, hurt by Alison's silence and lack of sympathy, but she couldn't stop talking about it. "But he never packed his things then, and this morning he showed up for his stuff. I demanded an explanation. He barely noticed me. When I stood in front of him to force him to look at me, he slugged me." She began crying. "Sure, we've had some bad fights, but he's never hit me."

Her soft sobs echoed in Alison's head, producing a dull buzz. Nina's tears were magnificent, the way they reflected the living room light and changed into golden drops traveling slowly over the curved surface of her face.

The room turned cold. Chilled currents of air swirled around Alison, brushing against her skin. Sound and sensation merged. Nina's voice was not nearly as interesting as the golden drops on her cheeks. As Nina wiped at her face the tears smeared into glistenind streaks.

"Will you ask Ben to talk to Stan for me?" she pleaded.

The liquid gold flowed faster, forming luminous spikes that hung from the edge of a white cliff and were illuminated by the glow from the ashtray.

*"Alison, I'm over here. Come here."*

*"I can't. Not now. Please."*

*"Follow me."*

*"I'm afraid. Please."*

*"There is nothing to fear. You'll see."*

*"Not yet. Give me more time. I need time."*

A tapping on her arm.

*"Your fear is unfounded. You can overcome it."*

"Alison, what's the matter?"

*"This way, Alison. Hurry. You must hurry."*

"Alison!"

She was being shaken.

*"Hurry, Ali."*

"Alison? My God, Alison, answer me!"

The golden drops faded.

"Alison!"

"I'm all right," Alison said, massaging her forehead. She felt so confused.

"What happened?" Nina was pale and trembling.

"I must have blacked out momentarily." The second time in one day, she thought, and the first time when she wasn't alone. She couldn't remember anything about the lapse. What was Nina doing there?

Ben rushed home when Mrs. Bruckner gave him Nina's message. From what he could piece together, Alison had practically chased Nina out the front door, assuring her that she felt better. Alison did not meet him at the door, and he was about to call her name when it occurred to him that she might be asleep. Walking upstairs, he heard water running. The sound came from the hall bathroom, the smallest of the three and the one Alison liked least. Passing the guest room, he noticed that the bedspread lay in a heap on the floor; the blanket had been folded over. The bathroom door was closed. He knocked.

"Ali, it's me." No answer. Then he realized that

water was seeping under the door. He opened it, and steam rushed into the hall. He burned his fingers on the tub faucet, grabbed a washcloth, and turned off the water. The master bedroom and his study were empty. Her car was outside, so she had to be home.

At the head of the steps, Ben smelled smoke. He ran downstairs, his heart pumping frantically. The smoke was coming from the kitchen.

"Ali!" he shouted.

She was standing near the sink, rock rigid. Despite the heat, her skin was freezing. He picked her up and carried her into the living room. Laying her on the sofa, he covered her with a heavy blanket and checked that her breathing was normal. He opened the kitchen windows and back door and closed the door to the kitchen. The cold air dispersed the smoke issuing in plumes from the broiler. He turned it off and found two charred steaks, which he assumed had been dinner.

Going back into the living room, he found Alison sleeping soundly. Drained, he collapsed onto the chair nearest her.

Alison awoke a few hours later to see Ben watching her. "How long have you been home?"

"A couple of hours. How do you feel?"

"Rested. I must have lain down for a minute and dozed off." She sat up with a start. "The steaks!"

"It's okay. They were too well done for us."

"Oh, Ben, I'm sorry."

"Don't be. We'll eat out tonight." He leaned toward her. "Ali, I want you to tell me exactly what happened." The question seemed to surprise her.

"Well, I put the steaks in the broiler and must

have dozed off." She held his hands. "How awfully careless. The house could have burned down."

"Not from a smoking broiler." He smiled.

"I'm good and hungry. Where shall we eat?"

"Your choice, but first, lie back down on the couch."

"Ben, I'm fine, honestly. How about driving into Boston for dinner?"

"Terrific idea. Now lie back." While Ali was asleep he'd debated with himself and finally decided that Pollack was right, he had to find out what had been going on during the last sessions.

"Ben, I'm starving."

He took the metronome from the piano and placed it on the coffee table.

"Ben, no. Please."

"Close your eyes."

"Can't we do this later?"

"Ali, lie back." He held firm against her protests, refusing to give in. "Listen closely to the ticking of the metronome. You are growing very tired. Each tick will rock you deeper and deeper into a relaxing sleep." It took him forty-five minutes to get her to a medium-depth trance.

"I'm going to ask you some questions. Even if some of them trouble you, you will answer them. You want to tell me exactly what you recall about our sessions. Do you understand?"

"Yes." Her tone was normal.

"During our sessions your voice is peculiar when you talk to me. Why is that?"

"I don't know."

"Are you aware that your voice is different when you speak to Stan?"

"No, it's not different."

Ben frowned. "Does your voice always sound normal to you?"

"Yes."

Try another tack. Be careful not to provide any clues. "Do your remember the induction technique Stan introduced in the past two sessions?"

"Yes."

"What was it?"

"He led me into a cave." There was excitement in her voice.

"Can you describe the cave?"

Alison supplied a remarkably accurate account, if his memory served him.

"Alison, you will tell me everything I want to know about the cave. You *will*, won't you?"

No response. He'd have to deepen her trance. "You are very tired. You crave sleep." Ben spent twenty minutes at it, periodically suggesting that she was willing, even eager to answer his questions concerning the cave.

"Do you remember the gardenias?"

"Yes. There were thousands of them."

"Why didn't you obey my order to pick one?"

"Nothing can leave."

"Why is that?"

She was silent. Again, he deepened her trance.

"What do you mean when you say that nothing can leave the cave?"

"It's Stan's rule."

"Stan *told* you?" Ben was astonished.

"Yes."

"How did he do that?"

"He told me."

"He *spoke* to you?"

"No."

"So how did he communicate with you?"

"He told me."

Ben was chilly. He got up to close the kitchen windows and the back door. The knot had returned in his chest. His mind raced, searching for explanations. Stan had created the cave fantasy, so, logically, Alison treated the cave and everything in it as Stan's. Therefore, picking a flower in the cave would be stealing.

Ben sat on the edge of the coffee table. "In our last session, Alison, you awakened spontaneously. What caused that?"

"Stan."

"Stan? He counted you out of the trance?"

"No. He led me out of the cave."

Ben realized that he mustn't let his bewilderment show in his voice. "Stan was in the cave with you?"

"Yes. We ran out of the cave together."

"Why?"

Alison began to stir, but Ben would not give up. She could resist him as much as she chose, but he'd work all night to get answers if he had to. For another hour he used the metronome, occasionally slowing its pace and patiently repeating soporific words. At last her breathing indicated that her trance had deepened. Then he considered his next move. It was a long shot, but he had to go for it.

"Did Stan ever deliberately disobey my orders?"

"Yes."

Her answer did not shock him, but her voice, emphatic, resentful, and defiant, did.

"Why did Stan resist?"

"You intruded." A hateful tone. Careful, he cautioned himself.

"Into the cave?"

"Our world. You are not welcome." Her answer hit him between the eyes, and they smarted. Pollack had noted that subjects under mutual hypnosis share intimately a common reality orientation. Their fantasy is jointly and solely theirs. But Ben would make her understand. He had to.

"The cave, Alison, is a fantasy. A world created through a trance. Fashioned purely from imagination. It has no existence—absolutely none—in reality."

Her hand moved from her chest to her side. She was only three feet from him, but suddenly he felt as if she were a million miles away. Emotions! He reprimanded himself. *He* was the hypnotist. He would demonstrate how unreal the fantasy was, no more than a figment of her imagination. For several minutes he let her rest, then he asked, "Do you see the gardenias?"

"Yes, they're beautiful." There was a recurrence of excitement in her voice.

"Smell them." She inhaled quickly. "You can smell them, can't you?"

"Yes."

"Touch them. Go ahead. Feel their velvety petals." Alison smiled. "Touch one particular flower. Single one out from the rest." Her right hand lifted and hung in the air. "Do you feel the petals?"

"Yes. They're cool."

"Caress the flower."

Her fingers explored the air.

"Close your hand around the flower. Cradle it."

Her hand had begun to close when for no apparent reason her arm dropped to the sofa.

"Alison, touch the flower. You want desperately to caress it."

Her hand rose slowly until it was about a foot from Ben's face. To destroy the fantasy, *he* had to dominate it.

"I order you to pick the flower."

Her arm quivered. "Nothing can leave." Her voice was faint, on the verge of cracking.

The knot was cutting off his breath. He must control the situation, overpower it. "Alison, this time *I* have hypnotized you. *I* have made the cave real. *I* have given the flowers meaning. You absolutely cannot disobey me. Pick the flower."

There was a rapping overhead, wood against wood. Ben glanced up at the ceiling.

"Nonononononononononononononononononono..." The echo was brittle, barely audible. Her face was flushed. From pain, he wondered, or fear? Her body twisted, then arched, her back lifting away from the cushions.

"I ORDER YOU TO PICK THE FLOWER."

"Nononononononononononononononononononono."

Louder rapping. A thumping against the floor in the guest room. Ben took the stairs two at a time. He quickly surveyed the room and found nothing unusual—except the icy air.

Fear and jealousy drove him on. He returned to the living room.

"ALISON, YOU MUST OBEY ME. PICK IT."

"Nonononononononononononononononononono." Her voice was fainter, yet shrill. Her fist flew at him, stinging his face. His heart drummed, his mind raced. No, it's impossible. Stan can't be with her. It's all in her imagination. Yet he had the sinking sensation that he was wrong.

"Is Stan there in the cave with you?"

Alison sat bolt upright, her trance rapidly fading.

"Alison, is Stan with you?"

He noticed the tic in her eyelid. Her mouth opened. She began breathing heavily. Running out of the cave? Ben lost control and grabbed her shoulders. "IS STAN WITH YOU?"

"YES." It came as an abrupt shout. Her eyes opened, and momentarily she did not recognize where she was.

Pollack had been right. Ben was in over his head and was ready to go crawling back for help.

# 18

Alison and Stan's minds were linked! Ben couldn't avoid that conclusion. If it were so damned impossible, then why did his heart ram against his lungs and cut off his breath every time he admitted to himself that Stan had an unnatural control over Alison's mind?

The thrust of the engines seemed to abate as the plane reached cruising altitude. Ben looked out the window at the snow-covered ground. Somewhere down there, Alison was worrying about her blackouts—as Ben was. He had set up an appointment for her with a good internist associated with the Massachusetts General Hospital and had made

Alison promise to keep the appointment. Ben had almost canceled his trip to see that she did. But—and he was ashamed to admit it—he was more preoccupied with his trip to North Carolina to meet Dr. George Stimson than he was with Alison's appointment. Besides, Nina would make sure that Alison got to the hospital.

As the land passed slowly beneath him, Ben mulled over the possibility that he was running away, distancing himself from his troubles. But he didn't really believe that. This trip was essential; Pollack had made that clear. He hated to leave Alison, but he had no choice. He hoped that Nina would not have her hands full.

The plane landed at the Durham airport two hours before his appointment with Stimson. The tension in Ben's chest spread through his body. He felt like a rubber band ready to snap at the slightest touch. To calm his nerves he went into the airport bar and ordered a Scotch. He purposely sat at a table near the entrance so he could watch the clock. In the rush that morning—arranging for a colleague to take his classes, asking Nina to stay with Alison, and getting to his flight—he'd forgotten his watch.

On Friday he had swallowed his pride and run to Pollack for help. They argued bitterly, Ben insisting that Alison's answers proved nothing, that they simply constituted her interpretation of what she *thought* to be true. Through a vestige of wakefulness, she realized that picking the flower was physically impossible, and the conflict his order created had jolted her from her trance. It was only natural for her to assume that Stan was with her in the cave. After all, he had introduced the cave in the first place, and it had become an integral part of their fantasy under hypnosis.

Pollack, of course, won the argument. There could be no doubt: Alison and Stan's minds were linked telepathically. He cited evidence extending back to the work of Anton Mesmer in the eighteenth century that hypnosis was a telepathically favorable state. Under other circumstances Ben would have scoffed, but he had scoured the libraries at Ardmore, Harvard, and Boston University, and through their parapsychological indices had found scores of papers that documented telepathy occurring between a hypnotist and his subject in trance. "Imagine how much more telepathically amenable *mutual* hypnosis is," said Pollack, cursing the fact that the idea had not dawned on him until the night he read the transcripts. "Ali and Stan are each other's *subject and hypnotist*." Pollack had easily won the argument.

In the taxi on the way to his appointment, Ben's hands shook so badly that he had difficulty reading Stimson's monograph. It didn't matter, he practically had the damn thing memorized. Pollack had dredged up the paper from one of the filing cabinets he stored in his den. Stimson had published other important monographs on extrasensory perception, but Pollack had lost contact with him and did not have the papers.

The taxi driver pointed out the Duke University campus, but Ben wasn't able to appreciate the scenery. He was too busy rehearsing his questions. Stimson had never experimented with mutual hypnosis, and he had been fascinated by Ben's idea of repeated volleys. It was a logical extension of his own work, but one that had never dawned on him. The taxi pulled up in front of the Physical Research Institute, several blocks from the campus. The red brick building was two stories high, surrounded by poplars and willows. Ben walked upstairs to Stimson's office.

From Stimson's deep, resonant voice over the phone, Ben had figured that he was tall, powerfully built, and about Pollack's age. But he was at least seventy, of slight stature, with a mane of silver hair, a contagious smile, and piercing blue eyes. Ben fidgeted while Dr. Stimson read scrupulously through the transcripts of the last sessions, hoping that he could provide a reasonable explanation. Pollack felt that if anyone could help, Stimson could. At last he finished the transcripts.

"Congratulations, Dr. West. In a way, you've topped my own achievements. I could kick myself for not having used mutual hypnosis in the novel way you have."

Despite his nervousness, Ben was flattered that Stimson appreciated his work.

"Dr. West, how has Alison been since you last hypnotized her?"

"Perfect. Very normal. You'd swear everything I mentioned about Stan's control was a lie."

"Not at all." Stimson smiled. "I'm not surprised." He had a soothing voice, a calm manner, despite his obvious energy. Considering his age, he seemed remarkably spirited. "I'd be more certain of my evaluation if I'd actually observed several sessions myself, but on the face of it I agree with Paul. Repeated mutual trances have forged subliminal bonds between Alison and Stan. Bonds they themselves are surely unaware of."

"Alison's unaware of them," Ben stated firmly.

Stimson perused the notes Ben had prepared on Alison's behavior and her responses during the last session, when he'd hypnotized her alone.

Stimson said, "From everything here, I'm convinced that Alison and Stan experience telepathy during their mutual trances. The larger issue is: Is their subconscious link strong enough to support telepathic communication while they're awake?"

"Is that possible?"

"Yes, and it could account for Alison and Stan's strange behavior."

Ben asked the inevitable question: "How can the link be broken?"

Stimson's perpetual grin broadened. "Dr. West, my attitude probably strikes you as strange, but you must realize that I've spent a lifetime working to *establish* telepathic ties between subjects. To be perfectly honest, I find it supremely ironic that I'm consulted to sever such connections."

"As long as we're being honest, I should tell you that Paul loaned me one of your monographs. Had I read it a few weeks ago, I'd have thought you were a fraud."

"Ah," Stimson sighed, "many people do." He got up from his desk and walked to the bookshelves. "Here—he gestured toward a row of binders—"is the past sixteen years of my life. I assume the monograph Paul gave you is the one I worked on when I taught at Ardmore. That's old stuff."

"You taught at Ardmore? Paul never mentioned it."

"In the fifties. Paul was my star student, my protégé. We were the department mavericks. The experiments in that paper were conducted at

Ardmore." He winked. "Unofficially, of course."

Ben was beginning to relax. Stimson's personality and candor were engaging. And despite Pollack's assurance of Stimson's reputation in his field, he was very unassuming. Still, Ben's anxiety gnawed at him. "The link can be broken, can't it?" he asked again. As he repeated the question, it dawned on him that he hadn't seriously entertained the possibility that the bond could *not* be broken, that the intangible thread between Stan and Alison could never be cut. Again, Stimson skirted the question. Ben added, "If you can forge them, you *can* break them." The statement was nearly a plea. Ben felt as if Stimson were his only chance to save Alison. He desperately needed his help.

Stimson moved toward the door. "Dr. West, before responding to your question—a very crucial question—let me show you something." Ben was almost frantic for an answer, but he politely followed his host down the hall. "I started out as a psychiatrist, teaching, and had a small private practice near Boston. By chance I stumbled onto the work of Vasiliev, a Russian physiologist and psychical researcher. In the nineteen twenties, Vasiliev discovered that he could hypnotize certain subjects even though he was miles away from them. He developed the theory that his hypnotic suggestions were transmitted by eletromagnetic waves, and for a time he was permitted to study this phenomenon.

"However, poor Vasiliev had no luck detecting his electromagnetic waves. And to his everlasting bedevilment, even when his subjects were locked in a room shielded from radio waves, he was still able

142

to hypnotize them and, incredibly, even transmit posthypnotic suggestions. At any rate, for lack of physical evidence, many Russian scientists decided that Vasiliev's research smacked of spiritualism, and he was forced to abandon it."

As they passed several laboratories, Stimson introduced Ben to his staff assistants, most of them younger than Ben.

"So you picked up where Vasiliev left off?" Ben asked.

"You'll see, Dr. West. What I'm about to demonstrate will help you put your own work in perspective."

"I don't need perspective," Ben muttered to himself, "but answers." Six hours had gone by since he'd left Alison, and he hoped she was all right. He'd telephone as soon as he could. His explanation for leaving was that a brilliant scientist at Duke was doing work similar to his and had invited him to fly down to compare notes. The invitation was just too good to turn down and another one might not be forthcoming if he did. Alison had encouraged him to go. In fact, she did not seem at all disappointed by his departure. But she did complain at Nina's arrival and accused Ben of treating her like an invalid. She seemed to regard his concern and his precautions insulting, saying they could use a rest from each other. Ben had given Nina his flight information and Dr. Stimson's phone number in case she had to reach him.

On the first floor, Stimson showed Ben into a room that was separated from the adjoining room by a glass panel.

"Dr. West, meet Kate, the love of my life." She

was a buxom woman—in her mid-forties, Ben guessed—and wore her thick chestnut hair piled in a bun on top of her head. She did not rise to greet him, but smiled and shook his hand. "Kate agreed to come in today so that we could show off for you."

"I appreciate it," Ben said.

Stimson closed the venetian blinds and turned on the lamp near Kate's chair. Swinging a pendant that caught the lamp's light, Stimson quickly hypnotized her. Ben had expected to see him hypnotize her at a distance—the subject of his monograph—and was disappointed by the conventional induction.

"She prefers the room to be dark when we start," Stimson said, opening the blinds. "I do everything to accommodate her."

Ben followed Dr. Stimson into the adjoining room. Kate faced the glass panel, her eyes closed. Stimson opened a valise containing twelve vials, each differently labeled: lemon, ammonia, rose, coffee, oregano.

"Pick one, Dr. West."

Ben selected ammonia, and Stimson uncapped the vial and sniffed. Immediately Kate wrinkled her nose and jerked her head to one side, as if to get away from the odor. Stimson took a deep breath, recoiling himself this time, and tears streamed down Kate's cheeks. Ben was dumbfounded. Did this mean that Ali...that Stan...? Stimson smiled at Ben's obvious confusion.

"Kate is in telepathic rapport with me only when she is in a trance."

Ben motioned to the vial marked coffee, and Stimson poured a few drops into his mouth. Kate smiled. Stimson spoke into the intercom. "What do you taste?"

"Coffee."

Ben couldn't help being awed by the seemingly unscientific basis of the demonstration. "How in the hell does she do it?"

Stimson said wryly, "If I knew that, Dr. West, surely I'd have won a Nobel Prize by now. All I can say with assurance is that Kate's ability to perceive telepathically depends on her state of consciousness. That is to say, in a trance, where the usual sensory stimuli are blocked out, another mode of perception emerges—but only when *I* hypnotize Kate. In her trance, her consciousness is so dependent on mine that she experiences whatever I do. I might add," he continued, "that it is not mutual. When I sit in that chair and Kate is in here, I'm a complete failure."

Ben's mind raced. Could Ali be aware of *his* thoughts? Could she tune into Stan's experiences? Stan, hers? Was Stan able...? Ben forced himself away from these torturous hypotheses. "Does Kate ever miss?" he asked.

"Oh, Lord, yes. Her accuracy depends on how sharp she feels, the time of day, things like that. For instance, she scores poorly at night but is very consistent in the morning. Interestingly, I cannot hypnotize Kate from a distance as I could the young man in the monograph you read. She must already be in a trance before anything paranormal can happen."

Ben shook his head. The significance of Stimson's work was seeping through his muddled mind. One person experiencing thoughts and stimuli directly from another human being. The ramifications were staggering. "Does Paul keep up with your research?"

"Not unless he reads the trade journals in my field. Watch this, Dr. West." Stimson heated a straight pin with a match, then pricked his finger. Kate's hand sprang off the armrest and landed in her lap.

"You pricked your left hand," Ben observed, beginning once again to relax and collect himself, "yet Kate moved her right."

Stimson beamed. "Yes, isn't it terrible? Another mystery. What's worse, there's no consistency to the hand she moves."

The old man was a calming influence. For some reason Ben had great faith in him. He had found his savior.

"This is going to sound ridiculous," Ben said. "Does Kate bleed?"

"No, but I'm working on it. I believe it'll happen with a great increase in rapport. Let me put it another way, Dr. West. Right now, Kate has a certain degree of rapport with me, but since I'm fully awake, I do not have equal rapport with her. Or, to use your charming expression, Kate and I do not share *mutual rapport*. Your mutual hypnosis protocol, Dr. West, is just the technique I've been groping for."

Ben asked, "Is there any chance you inadvertently leak sensory clues to her?"

Stimson laughed. "I threw this show together to impress you. However, when we score tests for statistical results, Kate is sealed in a soundproof, electrically shielded room. And I can even be traveling during the actual testing. It doesn't matter. Once I was in Jamaica."

"Jamaica?"

"Yes. I hypnotized Kate before going on vacation and instructed her to sleep for eight hours. On the plane and in Jamaica, I conducted several tests similar to what you've seen here. Kate responded to many of them." Stimson glanced sheepishly at Ben. "I didn't feel comfortable with my wife until the eight hours were up."

From Jamaica to Durham was about a thousand miles. Only three miles separated Cricket Drive from Sullivan Hall, where Stan now lived. Was Ali, at this moment, on Stan's wavelength? Was he manipulating her behavior? Ben forced himself back to the present and asked, "Do you have other subjects like Kate?"

"Unfortunately, no. Kate's one in a million. And it may be that in Ms. Kilmore and Mr. Fredericks you've discovered a one-in-two-million pair." Dr. Stimson closed the valise. "Let me show you one thing more, Dr. West."

Stimson closed his eyes.

Before Ben had counted to five, Kate woke up and waved at them through the glass.

Back in Dr. Stimson's office Ben asked, "Could the telepathic exchanges between Alison and Stan be as clear as those between you and Kate?"

"I doubt it. At least not yet. Kate and I have worked at this for eight years. Early on, Kate picked up only random fragments of my thoughts, which confused and frightened her. I had to learn to hold only one thought in my mind, and she had to learn to zero in on it. In other words, we were like a radio transmitter and receiver that had to be turned to the same frequency, otherwise the receiver picked up static. Alison and Stan have had no guidance in developing *control* over their telepathy. In fact, as I said earlier, I'm sure they don't even know it exists between them. It's functioning strictly at a subconscious level."

A research assistant brought in pastry and tea, and Dr. Stimson and Ben snacked at the desk. A change had come over Ben. His mutual hypnosis experiments, designed to break habituations, paled next to Dr. Stimson's achievements in telepathy. Anything would. Yet George Stimson and Paul Pollack both believed that mutual hypnosis could be more potent in establishing telepathic ties than conventional hypnosis. Ben wondered if his work with Alison and Stan was more momentous than anything he had dreamed of.

"I know I'm asking questions that at best have speculative answers, but what do Alison and Stan experience?"

Stimson shrugged. "Based on my experience with Kate, I'd have to assume that your subjects perceive snatches of each other's thoughts and daydreams. Random imagery from the other person's past. Possibly voices. Whatever, it must be very confusing for them—and terribly frightening. You can see where they might easily interpret their extraneous impressions as signs of insanity."

"Can you conjecture why Alison occasionally blacks out?"

"This is a guess, but I imagine that part of her mind becomes so absorbed in Stan's subliminal scenery that she loses consciousness; one reality wrenches her from another. Her blackouts are undoubtedly the periods when she and Stan are in strongest contact."

# LINKS

Ben glanced at the wall clock. His flight departed in less than two hours. He dared not miss it, but there were so many questions on his mind. And Stimson still had not indicated whether the link between Alison and Stan could be severed.

# 19

Ben's worst fears had been dispelled, dismissed by Stimson's hearty, assuring laugh. "A telepathic affair. Ridiculous! Dr. West, you read too much science fiction."

Ben reclined his seat. In an hour he'd land at Logan Airport. Stimson had convinced him that there was nothing dangerous or permanent in the telepathic bond between Stan and Alison. If Ben stopped the sessions, the bond would fade away in time. However, through continued sessions, Stimson felt that Alison and Stan could be taught to control their telepathy as he and Kate had. He explained that Alison's abnormal behavior was probably aggravated by the inadvertent secrecy Ben insisted on with his posthypnotic suggestion to forget everything that occurred during the sessions. This order had created tremendous subliminal conflicts in Alison, and probably in Stan too. In essence, they were communicating on a subconscious level, yet at the same time fighting to suppress awareness of their communications. Simply, Stimson concluded, Alison did not understand what was happening to her, so she interpreted the extraneous voices and imagery as signs of insanity. "Imagine, Dr. West, if you heard strange voices and had frequent fainting spells. You'd be afraid you were crazy too."

Stimson's advice was heartening. The first thing Ben had to do was to tell Alison and Stan what was happening between them and that Stan was attempting to control Alison's mind. Most important, Ben must instruct them to remember this explanation and everything about the sessions so that when they awoke Stan would realize what he'd done and Alison would realize that nothing was wrong with her. Remembering was the key. Knowledge was control.

"You've stumbled upon a gem of a discovery, Dr. West. My work with Kate will pale compared to the fluent, controlled telepathy Alison and Stan can be taught," Stimson had said. He was coming to Ardmore in a few days to show Ben how the degree of telepathy between Alison and Stan could be measured experimentally and what steps could be taken to have them control their communications. When Stimson had finished talking, Ben had visions of a Nobel Prize. At the very least.

Stuck in a holding pattern over Boston, Ben was impatient to land. He had only had time to phone Alison to tell her when he'd arrive. She had sounded all right. The doctor's tests had been negative. He couldn't wait to share Stimson's explanation with her. The pilot's announcement of clearance to land interrupted Ben's thoughts. This trip had been a lifesaver. Stimson had not only solved the mystery of Alison's spells, he had also given Ben the emotional distance he required as a scientist to appreciate the worth of his research and the weird and wonderful phenomenon he'd stumbled upon.

Ben walked down the ramp, scanning faces in the crowd.

"Hey, buddy, let me take the briefcase," Pollack offered.

"Where's Alison?"

"She's tired. She called to ask if I'd mind picking you up. I dropped Nina off on the way."

"Then Alison's alone?"

"It's okay. Nina says she's fine."

"Well, thanks for the lift."

"Don't mention it. Tell me about Stimson. Is he as active as ever?"

"Yes, indeed. And he'll be here soon to help me."

"That's great! It'll be fun to catch up with him, I suspect."

While Pollack threaded his way through traffic, Ben recounted Stimson's research with Kate and marveled at his incredible stamina.

"He's at least seventy-five." Pollack laughed.

"How come you didn't mention that he used to teach at Ardmore?"

"Those were the good old days, and frankly, I

prefer not to think about them. I live strictly in the present." Pollack cut short the discussion. Ben continued to talk about Stimson's research and how it elucidated his own work.

Pollack exclaimed, "That accounts for Ali's behavior this afternoon!"

Ben frowned. "You told me she was all right."

"Don't get excited, she's fine now. This afternoon about four Alison had a terrible headache and took some medication for it. She and Nina were watching television, and the pain got worse. Alison lay down on the sofa and complained that the noise from the television was unbearable. She became belligerent and irrational and began ranting. Nina was scared out of her mind. She called me and said that Alison was hallucinating and she didn't know what to do to calm her down. But when I arrived, she was sleeping like a baby in that canopy bed."

"You should have phoned me!"

"Easy, buddy. According to your timetable, you were en route to the airport."

"And you left her alone?"

"She's sound asleep."

Furious, Ben sat in silence as Pollack turned down Gurs Road, which connected with Cricket Drive. Getting out of the car, he said, "You shouldn't have left her by herself." Pollack drove away without answering.

Ben raced into the house. He had caused all of Alison's problems by using her in his experiment, and he owed it to her to solve them.

"I thought I heard the lock rattle. Welcome home," Alison greeted him.

"You're up. Is everything okay?"

"Yep. I'm heating up the leftovers of a roast Nina made. Sit down, dinner's about ready."

"What's this Pollack tells me about another spell?"

"Let's not discuss it right now. Let's just enjoy your being home and dinner. Nina's an excellent cook. I'm sick of the damn blackouts. I suppose it's a good sign that the doctor couldn't find anything."

Engage Alison in conversation, Stimson had recommended. Be certain she is alert and aware before you make your pitch.

"Have Nina and Stan made up yet? I haven't had time to talk to Stan like I promised Nina I would."

"No, he's moved out for good. Nina's very depressed about it, of course."

"Ali, I'm going to buy you that refrigerator you've been admiring."

"Ben, it's far too expensive."

"We'll budget after the wedding. I intended to surprise you with a wedding gift anyway, so it might as well be something you really want."

"The house is gift enough."

"Do my ears deceive me? Alison Kilmore turning down a present?"

She smiled and began stacking the dishes.

"I'll do that."

"No, just relax. I find it strange that we've talked about everything but your trip." She carried the plates to the kitchen sink. Her motions were slow but not sluggish. By then, Ben knew what to look for.

"Well, now that you mention it, we're going to have our first house guest in a few days," he said.

Alison scraped the leftovers into a plastic bag.

"Aren't you curious?" Ben asked.

"George Stimson, I imagine." From the refrigerator she took a glass bowl of fruited Jell-O. "When does he arrive?"

"The day after tomorrow. You don't mind, do you?"

"What's he like?"

"You'll love him. He's old, about seventy-five, and very spry. I'm sure he could outdo me at a day's work. He taught at Ardmore years ago."

"You're kidding. When?" The information caused the first spark of interest in her voice.

"In the fifties. He taught part-time and had a private practice. His research was a constant thorn in Hopkins's side. Pollack was his protégé." Approach the subject gradually, Ben cautioned himself. First, Stimson's work. Stimson advised him to make the facts credible. Just as Ben would have been skeptical about extrasensory perception, so Alison might turn off. Ben had to present Stimson's work in a rational, plausible light.

Alison brought the cream to the table. "Coffee?"

"One cup. I overdosed on coffee on the plane."

Alison boiled the water for coffee.

"Stimson conducted some pretty unorthodox experiments at Ardmore. He published them with a colleague affiliated with another university, which published their paper. Hopkins found out about it—Ali?" She was staring at the kitchen light reflected on the kettle. Avoid fixation, he recalled. Keep her occupied. "Ali, Stimson is into fascinating research. He uses hypnosis—"

"How long will he be staying?"

Keep her talking. Stimson said she can't drift if

she's talking. "Just two days. I should have checked with you before inviting him, but I was certain you wouldn't object."

"Why is he coming?"

He had planned to lay the groundwork first, before expanding on Stimson's research, but she was rushing him, and he couldn't jeopardize his and Stimson's credibility by lying. "Stimson's intrigued by our experiment. It's not so dissimilar from his own work."

"When will it happen?"

"What?"

"You intend to hypnotize me, don't you?" Her voice was flat.

"Honey, this is different. Not like the other night. The purpose of—"

"When?"

"Saturday." Find distractions, he thought. "What sights should we show Stimson?"

She turned on the faucet and began washing the dishes. She was growing lethargic.

"Ali, let's write down an itinerary for Stimson. You choose."

The plate slipped from her hand and broke in the sink. She wheeled around and shouted, "I can't. Please don't force me."

Ben held her. "Ali, listen to me." She stared blankly over his shoulder.

"No, I'm afraid." Her face turned pale.

"Ali, listen, please listen. There's absolutely nothing to fear." Ben felt as if he was pleading for his life. "I know now what's going on in your head. Stimson told me you're hearing voices or sounds. I'd be scared, too, if Stimson hadn't laid it all out for me. I can help you now, and so can he."

"Give me more time. Please. Not yet."

"Ali, concentrate on what I'm saying. Nothing's the matter with you. The sounds are real. The weird images you see are—"

She shoved him away, grabbed a water glass, and hurled it at the far wall. It flew past his shoulder and shattered against the refrigerator. Her eyes rolled back in her head.

"Ali!"

"LEAVE US ALONE," she screamed "GET OUT! GET OUT!"

"The cave! Jesus, you're locked into that fantasy!" Ben stared at her, heartsick.

Suddenly, the old jealousy raged in him, and he lunged for her. She evaded his grasp and made a dash for the living room, but he grabbed her and spun her around to face him. She slapped him across the face, which startled him, and he released his grip on her arm. Running through the hall, she tripped on Ben's briefcase and fell. Struggling to regain her balance, she reached for the telephone table and pulled herself up. The table toppled over.

"Ali!"

She shoved the table in his path. He caught her at the bottom of the stairs and wrapped his arms around her, pinning her arms to her side. Her body felt icy. Her breath chilled his face.

"Ali," he begged, "you must listen. To *me*. Not Stan. Whatever he's saying, he can't hurt you. I promise. Trust me. I won't let him hurt you. Please, let me help you."

She glared into his eyes. "Intruuuuuuu-deeeeeer . . . intruuuuuudeeeeeer . . . intruuuuuudee-eeeer . . ."

The echo ran through the hall, shocking Ben so

157

badly that he could move only to put his hands over his ears to block out the terrifying sound.

"Geeetooooouut . . . geeetooooouuut . . ."

Alison was indecisive, staring like a trapped animal first at the front door, then at the stairs. Ben backpedaled toward the door, and she ran upstairs.

"Alison," he yelled, "I can help you. I understand what you've been going through."

She stopped at the top of the stairs. "Leeeeaveeeuuuuusssaaallloooooooooooooooooooooo-ooonnne . . ."

Ben caught her on the landing. Her strength surprised him as she gripped his shoulders, her hands like vises, her fingers digging into his collarbone. She pushed him backward toward the steps.

"Ali, don't! It's me! Ben!" He could barely hear himself over the pounding of his heart. She was trying to kill him! This can't be happening, he thought. He fought with all his strength but could not wrench himself free. Alison forced him back over the balustrade. Then it dawned on him: Alison wasn't this strong, this wasn't *her* strength. "My God," he whispered, "Stan is somehow fighting me." He fell over the railing but managed to grab the banister and pull himself up.

"Ali!" he shouted.

"Geeeeetooooouuut . . . geeeeetooooouuut . . ."

Ben froze. it was Stan's voice.

"Intruuuuuudeeeeer . . . intruuuuuudeeeeer . . . intruuuuudeer . . ."

Unmistakably, Stan's voice rang out. Alison disappeared down the corridor. Ben chased after her, but he felt as if he were moving in slow motion. Complete panic had overtaken him.

"Ali, don't leave me for Stan." What was he saying? Stan controlled her mind. She couldn't help herself. When he flung open the door of the guest room, he found Alison sound asleep.

# 20

Stimson was dead wrong. Their telepathy was not vague and fragmented. Stan had clear, manipulating control over Alison's mind. And Stan wanted him dead.

Over the phone, Stimson balked at Ben's wild assertions. But when he calmed down and presented the events exactly as they had occurred, Stimson became deeply concerned. He advised against calling in a doctor, which he felt wasn't necessary, and to do nothing until he arrived. There were no more flights that night, but he would be on the first plane in the morning.

Pollack was either out or not answering his phone, so Ben braved the long night alone in a chair pulled next to the canopy bed. He retraced Alison's early fascination with the bed and her abrupt reversal that it be left in the guest room. It struck him how often he'd come home and found her napping in that bed, and he remembered the restless night he'd spent under the canopy, sensing a haunting presence. The strange rappings in the room, its bitter cold. These things had slipped his mind in his anxiety over Alison's blackouts, and recalling them filled him with a new horror.

At six the next morning. Alison awoke as though nothing unusual had happened. She showered and dressed and went downstairs to make breakfast. Ben stayed on her heels. She was unusually talkative and energetic until he broached the subject of Stimson's arrival. Then she grew detached, so he quickly dropped the subject.

While washing the dishes, he was startled by piano music. It was too resonant to be coming from their old radio. Running into the living room, he froze in mute terror: Alison sat rigid at the piano, her eyes glassy, playing with the skill of a professional. Numb, Ben moved toward the grand, but she remained oblivious to his presence. He was about to forcefully interrupt her playing when she stood up, passed within inches of his arm, and headed for the stairs. He waited for several minutes then followed her upstairs. She was out cold on the canopy bed. After several frantic calls, he located Pollack and asked him to pick up Stimson at the airport.

"Did you let her sleep in that bed?" Stimson asked, interrupting Ben's account of Alison's piano playing. He was pacing the living room.

"I stood next to the bed, uncertain what to do." He bit his lip in a gesture of revulsion. "This sounds silly, and I feel stupid admitting it, but I sensed Stan's presence in the room. Is that possible?" Since the incident, Ben had come to discount the probability that Stan's presence was only a figment of his imagination.

"That depends on whether you want a conservative or radical answer." Stimson sipped at a brandy; he was still chilled from the sudden change of climate.

"God, I want this nightmare to end!"

Stimson lit his pipe. "You say Stan does not play the piano?"

"Not that I know of."

"Find out for me. It's important. So did you leave Alison in the canopy bed or not?"

"No, I couldn't. Just the thought of . . . I don't know. What am I saying?"

"What were you feeling at the time?"

Ben walked over to the fireplace to warm himself. The crackling fire reminded him of the romantic evenings he and Alison had planned by the fireplace. Evenings that might never materialize. Their relationship was—no, had already—crumbled. Things would never be the same between them.

"Ben, surely you can describe your feelings."

Ben stared at the carpet. "Fear. Frustration. The inability to fight Stan because he was not physically present, though he was there just the same. And jealousy." Yes, his jealousy was very real. In some perverted way, Stan was more intimate with Alison than he could ever hope to be.

"Have you seen Stan lately?"

"I've avoided him like the plague."

"I can appreciate your position, but you'd be doing us both a favor to ask him about playing the piano. By the way, don't forget that Stan himself is not consciously aware of what he is doing to Alison. I'm sure of that." Ben did not look up; he was not so sure. "You mentioned that Alison tried to resist Stan's control, that she genuinely tried to fight off dissociation and contact with him?"

"Initially, yes."

"After her mind drifts, you cannot hold her responsible for her actions," Stimson reminded him.

*If* she was resisting. Ben wondered. One of Pollack's observations came to mind. "Buddy, you don't have any bad hang-ups. But Alison has a serious psychological problem. So can you blame her for preferring the serenity of the cave?"

"Pollack thinks it's possible that Alison prefers the peace of the cave to facing her psychological problems."

"Perhaps. Trance fantasies can be tenaciously real. How has Alison behaved since the incident?" Stimson asked.

"In the morning she's fine. But as the day wears on she gradually tires, growing quiet and introspective. Eventually she dozes off—to escape Stan's control, I suppose. But twice she's gone berserk, just before possession."

"Possession? Oh, come now, Ben, that's awfully

melodramatic. I wouldn't call it possession."

"What the hell would you call it?"

"Possession is a powerful word, fraught with all kinds of ugly implications associated with spirits or devils. In this case, both parties are very much human. Stan and Alison are experiencing a strong telepathic communication."

"When that communication is so binding that one person dominates the other, I call that possession," Ben insisted. "Alison did not try to push me over the banister, Stan did."

"I'm surprised to hear you making such unscientific observations," Stimson chided.

For a while they were silent, involved in their own thoughts. Then Stimson said, "I hope it won't be an imposition on you to arrange for the physiology laboratory and secure everything on my list. I plan to use some of the procedures I've developed with Kate to measure the degree of telepathy that exists between Alison and Stan."

Ben hesitated. After his experience the night before, he was afraid of having another session. He wanted the telepathic bond broken, not measured.

"Dr. West, trust me," said Stimson, discerning Ben's fear. "If their telepathy can be controlled, that must be done. You owe it to yourself and to science. Let's think of severing Alison and Stan's ties only as a last resort, one I'm sure we will not have to take. Now will you get the things on my list?"

"Yes, but I hate to leave you here alone with Ali."

"Don't worry about me. I may be old, but I can fend for myself." Stimson reached into his suitcase and held up a hypodermic syringe. "One hundred milligrams of Thorazine. And I've packed more potent drugs." He tapped the suitcase. "If she wakes up, I'm prepared." He walked Ben to the front door. "Does Alison have any recollection of her trance behavior?"

"None to my knowledge." Ben put on his coat. "I'll only be an hour. I don't think she'll awaken. In the past few days, she's slept for hours at a stretch. Incidentally, I haven't told her anything yet about what we'll be trying to do."

"Good," said Stimson. "For the time being, let's leave it that way. I'd prefer to chat with her first."

Ben hesitated at the door.

Stimson was amused. "Ben, I assure you I'll be alert for signs of trouble. And you *will* talk with Stan?"

"Yes."

Fifteen minutes after Ben's departure, Alison came downstairs. Stimson's presence startled her, but only momentarily. Introducing herself, she joined him on the living room sofa.

"You have a lovely house, Alison. My wife, Florence, would be so envious. She misses this area terribly."

"Ben says you once taught at Ardmore."

"Oh, it was a different university then. Conservative, but less conservative that it is now. And of course it wasn't as built up and didn't have nearly as many students. Florence and I lived not far from here."

"Near Cricket Drive?"

"Lord, yes. We used to visit the Goddards two houses down and go boating on the lake."

Ben was right. She liked Stimson immediately,

everything about him—his grin, his kind face, his soothing voice, his openness and warmth. Even the sharp aroma of his tobacco. She almost wanted to climb into his lap and have him hold her as her father never did. She smiled at this response, but still, she couldn't help wishing she had had a father like Stimson.

Alison stood suddenly. "I have something to show you. I'll be right back." She went to the pantry and studied the four cardboard boxes the movers had forgotten to take for Mrs. Wilson. Which was it? She opened the flaps of the second box. No, table linens. The first box, she remembered, contained stacks of letters bound in pink ribbons. She located the album in the corner box.

"This belonged to the former owners." She handed the album to Stimson and sat beside him on the couch. "I've been meaning to mail it to Mrs. Wilson. Did you know the Wilsons?"

"Yes, we met them several times through the Goddards, but when they moved away, we lost track." Stimson flipped several pages. "My lord, the Goddards!" he exclaimed. "I haven't seem them in—what?—twenty years." He turned to Alison. "You can't imagine what a thrill this is. Florence and I weren't big on taking pictures. It was a mistake; don't you and Ben make it."

It pleased Alison that Stimson was so delighted with the album. He found a snapshot of Dean Hopkins with hair and without his paunch, pointed out spots along the lake that had once been popular picnic areas, and identified Mr. Wilson—who definitely reminded Alison of someone, but she couldn't put her finger on it.

"He looks so familiar," she said. "Isn't that odd?"

"Didn't you meet him?"

"No, he died. That's why Mrs. Wilson gave up her house."

"Oh. I'm sorry to hear that."

"She went to her daughter's in Pennsylvania."

"Oh, my God." Stimson laughed, finding himself in a group shot. "Well, dear, now you see how cruel time can be."

"You've aged very gracefully," Alison said.

"What a sweet fib. Thank you." Stimson leaned over the coffee table to empty his pipe in the ashtray. "Florence doesn't look her age at all. She's as beautiful as the day I married her. She'd love to meet you and Ben. You must visit us sometime so that we can show you some famous southern hospitality."

Alison tried to block out the sound of his pipe rapping against the ashtray. It was giving her a headache. Stimson sat back, marveling over another photograph in the album. She scolded herself. For some reason it was taking a great effort to concentrate on the conversation and keep it going. She hoped she wouldn't do anything embarrassing, particularly because she liked Stimson so much. She excused herself and went upstairs to take her medication. The pounding in her head was building rapidly. She swallowed a double dose and checked herself in the mirror. She looked rested, though she had an urge to nap. Fighting it, she returned to the living room and tried to absorb Stimson's descriptions.

"The one on the left is Florence. I remember that afternoon so clearly, almost as if it were yesterday."

Alison focused on details to keep herself alert. Were there two or three people in the picture? Which one was Florence? The faces blurred. Concentrate, she warned herself. But the living room light was dimming. The photographs—and Stimson—appeared to be hidden behind a sheet of gauze. Hazy. Unreal. The pounding intensified, buzzing in her ears. Why isn't the medication working? Why? she thought wildly. The only clear object in the room was the ashtray. How beautifully it captured the dimming light and splintered it into golden rays, rays that bathed her in warmth, made her feel peaceful. But this peace, she had learned, was merely a prelude to fear.

"And look at this picture, dear."

She leaned closer to Stimson.

"No, this one, Alison. Here."

Which picture? Where? The page was gray.

"Alison, tell me how you feel."

Her eyes were drawn to the ashtray, and she could not—did not want to—free her gaze. The yellow light growing whiter was magnificent. She heard Stimson's voice from far away.

"Alison, look at this lovely snapshot. It's a restful scene. Imagine yourself lying on the dock, relaxed, not a care in the world. You are becoming sleepy. Very tired. The sun warms your entire body. It is a restful experience."

If only she could focus on Stimson, his words might make more sense. And he could prevent her from making a fool of herself.

"Feel the sun. It's making you sleepy. Very, very tired. Study the picture, Alison, and pay attention to my voice."

The light from the ashtray expanded to fill her vision; its tone flooded her ears.

"Dear, what a handsome ashtray. Was it a gift?"

Listen to him. He can help you. He may be the only one who can. She strained to respond. "Yes."

"From whom?"

Impossible to speak. No strength. No air. Answer him. "Stan." She realized she wouldn't be able to sustain the conversation much longer.

The ashtray moved, but somehow that didn't frighten her. It rose from the table and slowly floated before her, swaying back and forth in rhythm with the music. It was even more beautiful suspended in the air, reflecting light.

"You can hear me, Alison. No matter what else you are experiencing, my voice is penetrating. I am George Stimson. A friend. We like and understand each other. My voice is coming through to you."

His voice blended with the music and the shifting light. She had to follow its sweeping arc.

"The cave is real. It must be respected, dear."

"Yes." She was surprised she was able to speak.

"I'm aware that nothing can be removed from the cave. I will never ask you to do that."

"Yes." The light slowly moved in a circle now, soporific and melodious. But she had relaxed too much, had dropped her guard, and the fear was beginning to overtake her.

"You will not lose contact with my voice. No matter what happens, Alison, you will struggle to hear my voice."

With her last ounce of will power she shouted, "I don't want to go!"

"Go where, Alison?" Stimson swung the ashtray

in longer arcs, forcing her to turn her head continually to follow it. "Alison, concentrate on my voice," he said, blending the rhythm of his words with the motions of the ashtray. "You refuse to lose touch with me."

"Don't force me to go," Alison shouted, her palms pressed to her temples.

"Go where, Alison? Tell me. Where?"

"With them!"

"Them?" The answer startled him. He steadied his hands, then resumed the ashtray's rhythmic arcs. "Dear," he probed gently, "are other people in the cave with you?"

"Yes!"

"Alison, you must confide in me."

# 21

Upstairs, Alison slept, her body filled with enough Thorazine to knock her out for the night. To prevent her from dreaming—a mentation Stimson claimed was highly conducive to telepathy—he had administered one thousand milligrams of sodium amytal, shutting off her brain from any possible contact with Stan.

Ben sat in the kitchen, a cup of coffee in front of him, drumming his fingers against his thighs. Rain pounded against the porch roof and poured from the gutters. Why hadn't Stimson called yet? What did he expect to find on the tapes? Two hours had passed since Pollack dropped Stimson off at the campus to listen to the tapes for himself.

The high point of Ben's day had been not finding Stan. Admittedly, he'd made only a half-assed attempt. Confrontation between them would be pointless, he felt. It would only increase his festering enmity. So he had learned what he needed to know from Nina. Stan had played the piano through his high school years, but he hadn't had much time for it since starting college. That fact had not elicited any reaction from Stimson. Before he had gone to the campus office, they'd had an early dinner, an overseasoned salad and hamburgers burned on the outside and raw in the middle. Anyway, neither of them had been hungry. Stimson sat pensive, entrenched in his own thoughts not relaying much about his puzzling encounter with Alison. All he would say was that he had reappraised her predicament and concluded that the bond between her and Stan was unhealthy and dangerous. At this point, he and Ben were powerless to affect Stan's domination over Alison. The bond must be severed. But that's as far as Stimson would commit himself until he listened to the tapes. Irritated that Stimson was being so secretive, Ben was nevertheless gratified that they agreed with each other. Ben felt as if a tremendous burden had been lifted from his shoulders. Yes, he'd acted out of jealousy, but he'd assessed the situation correctly. He'd been right. In some strange way, Stan possessed Alison.

The technique required to destroy Stan's domination was unclear. "A piece of the puzzle is missing," Stimson had said without much elaboration, "a crucial ingredient that would complete the picture." Once Stimson figured it out, he would have a better idea of how to proceed. He thought Ben should be patient for a while longer.

Ben could not be patient, however, about the message Stimson had taken and which was resting near his coffee cup: Dr. Goodman called. Had Alison made up her mind about resuming appointments with him? Again, Ben gazed at the message. He was both angry and numbed by the fact that Alison had seen Goodman behind his back, that she had felt the need to see Goodman. What had she confided to Goodman that she felt she could not tell him? He had to know. He'd been putting off calling Goodman until he'd confronted Alison, but, restless and frustrated, he decided not to wait any longer.

Goodman's service answered. Ben hesitated and almost hung up, but then he left a message for the psychiatrist to return his call.

For the third time since Stimson had left, Ben went upstairs to the bedroom. By the hall light he saw that Alison lay on her back, her arms pressed against her sides. She seemed not to have moved since the injection. Her skin was pale, but that was better than the coronary gray it assumed while she was going through a spell. A spell! What a euphemism. All the horror and violence and mystery pigeonholed and tossed off as a spell. Just a spell.

As Ben sat on the bed, he couldn't help but wonder if somehow Stan was at this very minute controlling Alison's mind. The nagging doubt prickled his skin. Could Stimson be positive that in the delta waves of deep sleep Stan could not make contact with Ali? And once the link between Stan and Alison was broken, could Stimson—could anyone—be certain that the bond between them was totally, permanently severed? No. No one could guarantee that. Ben could never be sure. Every time he touched Ali, would he be reminded of Stan? The body is the shell, the person is in the personality. Would he interpret normal changes in Ali's behavior as Stan's influence? The questions rumbled around in his head, and he had no answers. How could he cope? How badly would all this damage his relationship with Ali?

Ben brushed Alison's forehead with his fingertips. It was cool, but not cold. Her drop in body temperature when she dissociated mystified him. Pollack's explanation, that it was merely a sign of her metabolism slowing down, seemed inadequate. Ben had experienced her icy breath and chilled skin, and then Stimson had, too. More than metabolic rates were involved. In fact, Stimson had lectured Ben for not informing him about Alison's drastic drop in temperature. He'd also castigated Ben for not mentioning the static on the tapes. And when he'd learned about it, he's insisted on hearing the tapes for himself. Ben hoped he had not overlooked any other vital details, potentially valuable clues. He was not the astute observer and, with Goodman complicating the picture, evidently not the sleuth of human motivation he'd prided himself on being.

Ben eyed Alison's dream diary on her night table. In the year she had kept it, he had respected her privacy; it was her wish. A silly one, since she told him everything—or he thought she had. He lifted the diary from the table and opened it at random in the dim light of the bed lamp. November 14, The drowning dream. The next two pages were blank. Then the fire dream. He read it. She had held back nothing from him; the description was familiar. He passed Thanksgiving and progressed page by page through early December. He recognized all of the dreams. Approaching vacation time, and their arguments about inviting her father to the wedding and visiting him, the frequency of the entries increased until, while they were in Bermuda, there were sometimes two a night. A marked change occurred after January 8, the evening following the first session of mutual hypnosis. Three blank pages. Then one entry. Then more blank pages. Nothing? He skimmed over the last few weeks again. On what date did Alison claim to have that nightmare, the falling dream? The session had been scheduled for a Friday, and on Wednesday he told her he was canceling that session. She protested, referring to the dream. So she'd had the nightmare on Tuesday, and there were no entries for any Tuesday. Or Monday. Strange that she had not recorded the dream. She obviously remembered it. Perhaps she simply forgot to note it in the diary. Ben wanted desperately to believe that.

Closing the diary, he noticed a piece of yellow paper tucked between two blank pages in the back. As he slipped it out, he thought he felt the bed move. But glancing down, he saw that Alison had not changed her position. The paper was a receipt from Saint Sebastian Cemetery in the amount of $2400. Ben was thoroughly confused. He pocketed the receipt and went downstairs.

Ben dialed the cemetery's number, but the line was busy. The fire had died, and the room was cold. With the poker he stirred the ashes, hoping to spark the few half-burned pieces of wood, but they would not rekindle.

He dialed again. Busy.

The cemetery, which was adjacent to Saint Sebastian's rectory, was nearby, no more than a five-minute drive from the house.

The line was still busy.

He tried to awaken Alison, but she was out cold. He disliked leaving her, which was why he hadn't listened to the tapes with Stimson. But he couldn't help himself. There was no way she would wake up. Even if Stimson called, the phone would not disturb her. He put on his coat, got his umbrella, and checked on Alison one final time. She had rolled over on her side and was sleeping soundly.

He double-locked the door just in case Stan got any funny ideas. The rain cascaded off the car windshield, hampering Ben's visibility. Reflections of highway lights rippled across the road. He strained to guide the car along the white dividing markers and stay on the road. Several times he felt inside his pocket to make sure he had the receipt.

He turned onto Webster Avenue and saw Saint Sebastian's steeple in the distance. Beyond the church was the rectory. He drove through the cemetery's main gate and under the intricate arbor. The path was laid in serpentine sections past the smallest headstones, then, approaching the center of the grounds, the trappings of burial grew grander. Ahead, Ben noticed the outline of a building; the ground floor was lit.

He left his umbrella in the car and raced to the door, which was covered by a slim portico.

There was no answer.

He knocked harder.

The door was opened by a man about twice Ben's age wearing overalls. "Yeah, wadda ya want?"

"I'd like to speak with you for just a few minutes."

"I'm on the phone. Besides, we're closed. Can't ya read?" He gestured at the weekly schedule tacked to the door.

"This is urgent." Ben paused. "You can at least let me in out of the rain. I won't take much of your time."

The man stepped back. "Come on," he said, irritably. "Don't want the heat to escape. The cheap bastards shut it off when they go home. I'll tell my friend I'll call back."

When the man returned, Ben handed him the receipt. "Can you tell me what this is for?"

"Mister, it sure ain't for groceries." He laughed coarsely, then glowered at Ben. "Why do ya wanna know?"

"It's important, I assure you, that I know what was bought and who made the purchase."

"That's confidential stuff," the man answered.

"My name is Benjamin West, Dr. West." He showed his university identification card. The man studied it before motioning Ben into an office cluttered with wilted wreathes and cardboard vases containing dead flowers.

"Have to find the invoice number. No date on receipts." The man ran his finger down several rows of figures in a ledger. "Here it is," he said. "Now I gotta get the invoice."

"What's the date of the purchase?" Ben asked.

The man glanced again at the ledger. "Week ago yesterday."

Before he had flown to Durham. Before Alison— no, Stan—had tried to kill him. Did one, or both of them, really intend to murder him? Ben's hands began to shake a little, and he stuffed them in his coat jackets.

"Here we go," the man said. "For a plot. Big one. Name of West." The man stepped toward Ben. "You okay?"

Ben's throat was dry, pinched at the back. It hurt to swallow. Blood surged in his ears as if to intentionally drown out the answer to his next question. "Who purchased it?" he managed to ask.

"Ya hard a hearin'? I told ya. West. Gal by the name of West. A real looker." He winked. "A bit tipsy, though. Some folks can't take cemeteries without a belt in them." He looked quizzically at Ben. "Hey, didn't you say your name is West?"

"Yes."

The man tilted his head. "Your wife, huh?"

"Yes, my wife." Ben gazed at the invoice. "Did she mention why she was buying a plot?"

"Oh, yeah! She's gonna hold one of them society teas. Wants a quiet atmosphere." He laughed.

"I mean, did she say who the plot was for?"

The man, still chuckling over his remark, lifted the blue carbon of the invoice in a second ledger. A white sheet was stapled to it. "Looks like there's been a mistake." He read the white sheet carefully. "Your wife bought two small plots. At this price, they'd be up near the front of the cemetery."

Ben's lungs rammed against his ribs. Were they planning to murder him and Stimson? Ben quickly realized he was being ridiculous. He forced out the question: "Who are they for?"

For the first time the man regarded Ben suspiciously. "This have anything to do with the cops?"

"No, of course not."

"It don't say here. But weights were ordered."

"Weights?"

"Yeah. Tombstones. Means your wife had to write out the inscriptions she wanted."

"Where would that record be?"

"In the shop."

"May I see it?" The man's reluctance was obvious. "Please. This is very important."

Ben followed him across the hall and down a flight of stairs illuminated by a small red bulb. The man threw a switch that lit a large workshop filled with marble stones, most of them rough and uncut. Cutting and polishing machines were clustered in the middle of the shop.

"Stay here," he said. "You could fall over somethin', and I'd be responsible." He inspected the pink slips attached to each headstone. "Here we go." In an instant, Ben stood next to him. "I warned ya," he growled. "I could lose my job for this."

Ben stared at two rectangular stones, their tops and sides rough gray, their fronts polished to a high luster. "I do nice work, huh?" Ben was speechless. The stones were for Alison and Stan and showed that they would die on March 16. That's three days from today, he realized.

Jesus! Stan's not after me at all, Ben almost whispered aloud. They're going to kill each other! A suicide pact!

"You okay, Dr. West? Guess most folks ain't used to being around this stuff. Fresh air'll make you feel better. I've been doin' this for years. Even the stiffs don't bother me."

Ben started for the stairs.

"Today's the thirteenth. Don't worry, I'll have

the inscriptions ready in time." He trailed Ben upstairs. "Patients?"

"What?"

"Kilmore and the Fredericks fellow. Guess they're your patients."

Ben crossed the hall to the door.

"If you don't mind my askin', wadda they got?"

Ben's answer was automatic, flat, the first thing that popped into his head. "Cancer." He ran to the car.

The man watched him from the doorway. "Spooky how you can tell just when they're gonna die."

# 22

It had been many years since George Stimson was so excited. At first he had been dubious because it was such a long shot, even for a man like himself who dealt regularly with paranormal phenomena.

His heart pounding, he had analyzed the tapes in the university's electronic lab after playing them in Ben's office. He knew he had to talk with Stan. The rain had not let up, and to keep the tapes dry he wrapped them in an envelope and slid them inside his suit jacket.

What was the name of Stan's dorm? Simpson? Sullivan? One of the old dorms. He kicked himself for not remembering which one Ben had mentioned.

Well, he never could keep them straight, even when he had taught at Ardmore.

Ben should have told him about the hum long before now, perhaps when he'd telephoned or visited in Durham. Precious days had been lost. Despite the urgency of his mission, Stimson purposely walked slowly to calm himself. He was also preoccupied with his awesome discovery. He couldn't stop smiling and shaking his head at his good fortune. The students who passed by probably thought he was senile.

The noise on the first few tapes was uninteresting, constant and unmodulated. But on the last two tapes the hum had fluctuations and was sporadic. He was no linguist, but even on first hearing the tapes he recognized immediately the cadence of human speech. The hum had to be a Raudive voice phenomenon, it had to be—subconscious communications psychokinetically spilling themselves onto the tapes. The Latvian psychologist Konstantin Raudive had documented such a case in the 1960s. There were other less well investigated cases, and as Stimson had listened to the tapes in Ben's office, he'd been cautious about hoping he'd stumbled across the best case yet. He'd replayed the last two tapes several times and was convinced the patterned hum represented telepathic exchanges between Alison and Stan. That would have been a momentous find in itself. But, on electronically deciphering the hum, he had made an even greater discovery.

Two girls in yellow slickers approached.

"Excuse me," Stimson said.

They seemed not to hear him and hurried by in

the rain. Stimson caught up with them.

"Excuse me."

"Yes?" asked one of the girls.

"Could you direct me to a particular dormitory? Simpson or Sullivan?"

She pointed across the campus. "Sullivan. It's down there. The building closest to the library."

He thanked her. He expected that Stan would be in on a night like this. But still he did not rush. He'd put the collar of his raincoat over his head, and that kept him dry enough. It would do no good to get overexcited. Next to his chest rested proof of a rare phenomenon far more staggering than anything he'd ever dreamed of discovering. He shook his head once again over his splendid luck.

The electronic lab tests had been relatively easy. The human voice contains frequencies between three hundred and three thousand cycles per second, and he'd measured the hum frequencies on the tape between eight thousand and nine thousand cycles per second. After he had determined this range and filtered the hum frequencies from the normal voices, he transferred the sounds to a fresh tape. At that stage he was certain of the speech cadence, convinced that the phrasing and pauses of varying lengths represented speech. From that point it was only a matter of electronically shifting the spectrum down to the normal voice range. The narrow frequency span made the voices thin and mechanical but discernible enough. Under hypnosis and in the cave, Alison no doubt heard the voices clearly. But in a waking state, Stimson's hunch was that Alison's communication from Stan and the others sounded like the tapes, shrill and static. That awful noise helped to explain her headaches and fear. Imagine having that terrible noise in your head.

Stimson passed the library and entered Sullivan Hall. He needed one more fact, one additional piece to complete the puzzle. Students milled around in the lobby. One of the students standing by the Coke machine gave him instructions—fourth floor, left corridor. He didn't know the room number, but someone on that floor would. Too bad they didn't install an elevator in the dorm, Stimson mumbled to himself as he began climbing the stairs.

Funny how he had not been shocked by the voices. Their pleas, persuasion, cajoling. And all that concern with fear. In fact, once he realized what he was listening to, his only emotion had been profound awe. He had been able to transcribe an incredible dialogue from the original tapes. Where words were not crystal clear, Stimson guessed at them. *Alison, this way. Follow (me)*. Stimson suspected that this was Stan's voice until he deciphered Alison's response: *I can't, Mother. Don't (insist). I'm frightened.* The most supplicating squeals, Stimson concluded, were Stan's: *You must (not) be afraid. It is (unwarranted). Believe me, Ali. Come (with) me.* That voice repeatedly encouraged Alison to play the piano: *It will comfort you, Ali. Help you overcome your (fear).* Stimson deduced that the piano playing was Stan's means of focusing Alison's concentration before he began his coaxing. There were other voices on the tape that Stimson had no way of identifying.

At the first landing, he stopped to catch his breath, the tapes clutched tightly to his heart.

# 23

My God, where was she!

Ben raced frantically from room to room shouting Alison's name. With so much Thorazine in her system—at least twelve hours' worth—how could she have awakened? Where would she have gone? At the kitchen window, he jerked back the curtain—her car was missing from the driveway. How could she have been alert enough to drive?

The ride to the campus never seemed so long, every turn a delay, every car and traffic light an obstacle. If an intersection was fairly deserted, Ben sped right through the light. If something had happened to Ali he's never forgive himself. Whatever information he'd wanted from the cemetery could have waited until morning or until Stimson had gotten back. Damn it!

Ben turned onto Lancaster Pike, which led directly to the campus. His mind was clouded. He was making assumptions. Because Ali wasn't at the house did not necessarily mean that she had left of her own volition. Perhaps Stimson had figured out a solution for disconnecting the link between Alison and Stan and, with Pollack, had taken her back to the campus to begin. No, that was wishful thinking. Ben had to face the very real possibility: Stan. But why, then, was Ali's car missing?

Pulling into the university parking lot, Ben spotted Alison's car at the end closest to Sullivan Hall. His throat tightened. For an instant he hesitated, wishing Stimson were with him. Hurrying across the lot, he counted windows—up four, over three. A light shone in Stan's room. Suddenly the campus loomed up before him. Buildings merged with the darkness to form a vast prop studded with thousands of tiny square lights. In one of those squares . . . He shuddered. An institution of learning filled with so much ignorance.

In his haste, he'd forgotten his umbrella in the car, and hail beat against his raincoat and slipped under his collar.

He still did not comprehend Alison's behavior. Was her desire to escape reality so strong that she was willing to die to attain whatever fantasy Stan promised her? What did that imply about how Ali really felt about him and their marrage? Could a person will himself to die? Sometimes a terminally ill patient did, he was well aware. A rat experiment he'd read about flashed through his mind. The rats had been conditioned to slow their heartbeat in return for electric shocks to the pleasure centers of their brains. Many rats, greedy for pleasure, stopped their hearts and died. Could man's desire for pleasure dominate his instinct for survival? Could people exposed to a majestic, serene fantasy, as Alison had been, be persuaded to flee this world whatever the cost? Was Ali even conscious of the fact that she risked death? Maybe Stan was tricking her in some way.

Shunning the curved pavement, Ben took a short cut across the part of the quad that sloped up toward the dorm. The ground was a puddle of mud that sucked at his shoes harder, the faster he tried to move. As he drew closer to Stan's window he looked for shadows, a sign that they were there together. Hail showered his face, forcing him to squint. How his life had changed. Disintegrated from a promising future to a macabre affair where another man possessed his love. And all for a goddamn experiment. He had made a terrible mistake by including Ali in the sessions, and would have given anything to take back the past two months and start again. In a fury, he rushed along the hedge separating the quad from the dorm until he found the passageway burrowed through the hedge by streams of students over the years.

The dorm was crowded with students, all impeding his progress. Some were in his classes and tried to talk to him. He weaved among them, bounded up the four flights, and pounded on Stan's door. There was no answer. He rattled the doorknob and was surprised when the door opened.

Stimson was sprawled on the floor. Blood had clotted over his left eye and mouth. A chair had been overturned. Ben put his hand on Stimson's chest. He was alive.

Ben was suddenly aware of the students milling in the doorway.

"Get a doctor," he shouted. A student ran to the hall phone to call the infirmary.

Stimson moaned and moved his head.

"Can you talk?" Ben asked, his forehead creased with concern.

Stimson opened his right eye.

Ben wet a washcloth in the bathroom and gingerly wiped the blood from Stimson's face. There was a bad gash above his eye and two gashes on his upper lip, as if he'd bitten it. His breathing was labored as he tried to speak. Ben snapped at the students who had filtered into the room.

"Out. Everyone out. And close the door behind you. Bring the doctor as soon as he gets here."

No one moved.

"Get the hell out this second or I'll have all of you suspended."

They backed out slowly. Ben slammed the door.

"Is it all right if I help you onto the bed? Maybe I'd better wait until the doctor comes and examines you."

Stimson, nodded and tried to sit up. Ben helped him to his feet, shouldering most of his weight, and laid him on the bed.

"What happened here?" Ben asked.

Stimson spoke with difficulty. "We were talking about the tapes when Stan lapsed into a daze. I tried to maintain contact with him by asking him to include me in his fantasy, share it with me. It had worked with Alison. But he attacked me."

"Alison hasn't been here?"

Stimson's eyes widened. "But the drugs? She's missing?"

"Stay still. The doctor will be here any minute." Stimson's talking had caused his lip to bleed. Ben patted the blood away with the washcloth.

"No, Ben." Stimson pushed his hand away. "It's imperative that you find Alison before Stan does."

The doctor arrived and Ben rushed outside. If they're already together they'd look for privacy, Stimson had warned, a place where they wouldn't be interrupted. Where? Campus buildings, halls, rooms, basements, flashed through Ben's mind. Privacy. Someplace where they wouldn't be disturbed. He scanned the campus in front of him, feeling a deep pang of hopelessness. How many secluded corners were there? Think! Think! With the Thorazine in her, Alison probably isn't too steady, might not wander too far. Someplace close by. Isolated. Yes! The cubicles. He started across the knoll toward the library.

The cubicles were a series of private rooms that ran around the periphery of the library's third floor. Each graduate student had his own room and key. Stan had forfeited his cubicle when he completed his coursework, but Alison had one that she used when she wanted to study alone. The cubicles along the south hall were dark. Ben rounded the corner to the east wing. Alison's room was midway down the corridor.

The lights were out and the door locked. It was impossible to see through the milky glass window. He banged on the door. "Ali!"

The door to the adjacent cubicle swung open and a gaunt student peered out. "What's up, Dr. West?"

"Have you seen Alison?"

"No."

"How long have you been here?"

"About ten minutes."

"Stand by this door. Don't budge."

The master keys were kept by the librarian on the first floor. She gave Ben an argument. The cubicles were private; not even professors could enter without the consent of a student. Those were the rules, and he knew it. Ben grabbed the set of keys from the desk and headed upstairs, the librarian protesting after him.

The cubicle was empty. He switched on the desk lamp. A thin layer of dust coated the desk. Alison had not used this room for some time.

"Is something the matter with Alison?" the student asked.

Ben handed him the keys. "Return these."

The hailstorm had stopped. Impatiently Ben shifted from one foot to the other on the library steps. Think! They wouldn't hide in any of the buildings where night classes were in progress. That eliminated quite a few places. He counted on his fingers the number of buildings that were likely to be deserted at that hour. Of course! The renovated wing of Austin Hall! Stan would figure that he'd never think to look for them there. He sped toward the building.

The second and third floors had been practically

gutted and were sealed off with flimsy partitions. As he came up the back path to Austin, he stopped dead in his tracks. The light was on in his office. He raced as fast as he could up the steps and through the circular foyer. He almost barreled into Hopkins on the second landing.

"West!"

Ben kept going.

"West! What's the rush?"

Ben's footsteps echoed in the empty hall. "I might need your help," he yelled over his shoulder without breaking stride. His office was the last room, a mile away. Hopkins's voice rang out again, closer this time, but Ben did not slow down.

As he scrambled around the final corner, he saw through the translucent window of his office that his desk light was on. Had he left it on? No, the janitor would have turned it off. He was gasping for breath; his lungs ached. He burst into his office, the door slamming against the wall. Alison and Stan sat in their customary places in the center of the room. The third chair, the one Ben used, had been pushed aside. Their bodies sagged as if melted by waves of undetectable heat. They were not sitting in the chairs so much as draped over them.

Ben rushed to Alison and felt her pulse. Her skin was freezing. Ben grabbed her shoulders and straightened her up.

"Ali, listen to me!"

The muscles in her face tightened.

"I know that you can hear me. Just listen. Please."

Her body stiffened. Thank God he was getting through to her.

"West, what the hell's going on here?" Hopkins panted. He couldn't believe his eyes.

"Ali, I love you. Very much. Don't leave me for Stan. You don't have to obey him."

Her body writhed. The frustration on her face was palpable.

"West, what is this? What are you saying?"

Alison's mouth sagged. "She is mine." Stan's voice! "She's coming with me."

Hopkins turned white. "Jesus," he murmured. "West, what the hell is going on?"

Ben violently shook Alison. "Ali, you are going to die for a *fantasy,* for a figment of your imagination, for something that exists only in your mind. Do you understand what I'm saying? Listen to *me,* not to Stan. I can guide you out of the cave to safety."

Stan's voice again. "She has chosen to come with me . . . comewithme . . . comewithme . . . withme . . . withme . . . memememe." Hopkins covered his ears at the eerie, piercing sounds. Ben realized that Stan was whisking her deeper into the cave. And fast.

"West," said Hopkins blankly, "West."

Ben drew back his arm and threw his body into punch that smashed against Stan's face. Stan's head bounced back like rubber hit with a hammer. His chair teetered backward.

"You will not take her with you, you bastard," Ben screamed. "I'll kill you if I have to to save her." His second punch knocked Stan to the floor. Ben lunged at him, pliant and defenseless. Wrapping his hands around Stan's throat, Ben heard Stan's echo behind him, "Helpushelpushelpus . . ." The echo grew fainter, more distant. They had traveled farther into the cave.

Hopkins tugged at Ben's wrists. "West, for God's sake, what are you doing? Have you gone mad? You'll kill him." He wrenched Ben's hands from Stan's throat. Ben knelt beside Alison's chair. He could feel tears welling in his eyes.

"Ali, don't be afraid of Stan. This fantasy is not worth death. I know all about the plots you bought at the cemetery. You don't have to die. The beauty of the cave, the peace you feel there, are illusions." His voice cracked. Tears burned his cheeks. "I love you, Ali. I love you so much."

Her body squirmed and fell forward. He caught her in his arms. Was she trying to shrug off Stan's control? So she could hear him better he whispered into her ear. "This is Ben. Don't die, Ali. Don't be scared of Stan. He can't hurt you now that I'm here. Your life is here with me. We'll solve your problems together, I promise." He picked her up in his arms and hurried out of the office.

"West," Hopkins shouted, "where are you taking her? What about Fredericks? Come back here and explain to me what in the hell is going on. West!"

# 24

At home again, Ben failed to awaken Alison. Sitting on their bed, he pleaded with every argument he could think of to arouse her until his thoughts grew muddled and irrational.

Stimson called on the chance that Ben had located Alison and returned home; he was relieved that Ben had found her. He tried to calm Ben by assuring him that she would eventually wake from her trance. Ben told Stimson what had happened in his office, then thought to ask Stimson how he felt. He was all right and decided to check on Stan. Ben gave him directions.

Ben returned to the bedroom. Alison's waning

pulse and drop in temperature panicked him. Was he going to lose her after all?

Stimson called again, this time from Ben's office. Hopkins was having some sort of fit. Without explaining too much, Stimson had introduced himself and was taking Stan to Clifton Hospital. He'd sworn Hopkins to secrecy by assuring him that he was a good friend of Ben and Paul's and by promising to explain everything later. Stimson had also contacted Paul, who agreed to meet him at the hospital. Stimson used to know Bloser and Minsky there, and he told Ben to bring Alison to the hospital. As he hung up, Stimson prayed that Bloser or Minsky was still around. If not, the hospital surely wouldn't turn away two patients in dire need of medical attention.

Alison and Stan lay in adjacent hospital beds, illuminated by the dull light of early morning. IVs stuck in their arms dripped saline solution into their blood.

Though exhausted from the hellish night, Ben just couldn't sit still. He paced in front of the window as Stimson and Pollack set up the EEG equipment.

Ben could not stomach the sight of Stan. His expression of peaceful innocence was not innocuous, as Stimson contended, but a mocking smile of victory. There was malevolence in Stan's passivity. Why didn't Stimson admit it? Ben had fought to prevent Stan from being in the room with Ali, but Stimson had insisted. It was much easier for them to measure Stan's effect on Alison if they both stayed in the same room. Stimson had had the last word:

"Ben, at this point their physical proximity is the least of our worries."

Stimson's connections at Clifton Hospital were a godsend. A large metropolitan hospital would have asked embarrassing questions, demanded that their own physicians take charge. At rural Clifton, Stimson had been fondly remembered and was allowed to assume care of Alison and Stan.

When their pulses began slowing down, Stimson had administered amphetamines, which failed to arouse them, and he would not experiment beyond a safe dosage. Barbiturates, on the other hand, might impede the communication between Alison and Stan, but they would also exacerbate their condition.

Gently parting Alison's hair, Stimson pasted silver electrodes to her head and ear. Despite his fatigue and the fact that his left eye had swollen shut, Stimson moved adroitly. He felt responsible for what had happened and had apologized several times to Ben for not coming directly to him with his conclusions based on the tapes. Ben brushed aside Stimson's apologies, realizing that the sole responsibility and guilt for everything that had befallen Alison was his alone.

When Pollack finished wiring Stan with electrodes, Stimson switched on the electroencephalograph and began tracking Alison and Stan's brain waves.

"Ben." Stimson motioned toward the chart rolling tediously from the machine. Preoccupied, Ben had tuned himself out. The night's events were an incomprehensible blur. The date, March 16, flashed in his mind. When on the sixteenth?

Morning? Evening? He had to figure out how much time remained, for he had no longer even a lingering doubt that Stan intended to die and take Ali with him. How would he do it? Or was he staring at that answer right now?

"Ben," Stimson repeated. The chart was coiling onto the floor.

This time Ben heard Stimson but ignored him. He felt dazed. His nerves were raw with guilt. Oh, God, what had he done? If Alison survived, would she ever forgive him?

"Ben," said Stimson urgently.

Ben turned, focusing on Stimson's swollen lip and purple eye. He hesitated; he wasn't sure he could tolerate another shock.

"Pull yourself together," Pollack reprimanded him. "You've been no help whatsoever for the past few hours. Now look at the chart," he said sharply.

Ben read the inked lines on the graph. Alison and Stan's brain-wave patterns were identical: rippling theta waves, three to seven cycles a second, waves characteristic of yogis and Zen monks in the very deepest states of meditation.

"I've never observed anything like it," Pollack said, his voice filled more with amazement than concern. "They're not actually in a trance at all. They're suspended in a reverie and sharing it as though they were one and the same person."

Ben prayed for a break in the synchronous pattern, but the lines continued to parallel each other.

"Separate them," he demanded of Stimson. "For the love of God, sever the bond between them!"

"We will, Ben, we will."

"How? Tell me how, damn it!"

Stimson didn't respond.

Glaring at Stan, Ben swore at him silently. I'll kill you if I have to. You can count on that.

Stimson touched Ben's arm. "You need a break. I'll keep you company. Paul won't object to minding the store." His attempt at humor was weak. At the door, Stimson instructed Pollack not to let anyone read the chart. "If a nurse, doctor, anyone, comes nosing around, just say the patients are recovering from a drug overdose. That's all."

Stimson wondered how much longer this tragedy could be kept secret. He'd lied to Bloser, telling him he wanted two students who had overdosed admitted under his care. When Bloser arrived, he'd have to be told the truth.

At six A.M., Clifton Hospital was quiet, manned only by a skeletal night staff. But they went off duty in an hour, and the full staff would shortly be poking around in their business.

In the doctors' lounge, Stimson tentatively sipped at his coffee, wincing as it hit his lip. "Sit down, Ben. Your pacing makes me feel guiltier, if that's possible." Stimson needed time to collect his thoughts. He still had no idea how to break the bond between Alison and Stan.

"You!" Ben said. "Why should you feel anything but contempt for my towering stupidity! And compassion for Ali." Ben slammed his fists against a vending machine. "Why is she in such pain? Did you notice the expression on her face? What in the hell is he doing to her?"

"Sit down, please, Ben. Alison's expression is not due to pain, if that's any consolation. I believe it's caused by fear."

"Fear? Of what, the cave fantasy?" He was confused.

"I have a strange tale to relate that will explain the missing piece of the puzzle." Blood trickled from his lip, and he dabbed at it with his handkerchief.

Ben sank into a chair, overcome by a sense of utter despair. "Alison's going to die," he blurted out. Then he informed Stimson of what he had learned at the cemetery. "What does it mean? Why is Stan trying to kill her? How can she possibly know when she's going to die?"

"We can't be sure that she does. We can only assume she's following Stan's instructions. I was able to filter the hum on the last tapes. It's voices—"

"Voices?"

"That I was able to decipher. Stan's is one of those voices. Alison's mother's is another."

The color drained from Ben's face. "It's not possible, not possible."

"Once I decoded the tapes, I realized there was still a part of the puzzle missing. And then I had the answer. Seven years ago, one of my lab assistants, Elvira, died."

"But—"

"Yes, you met her in Durham, but seven years ago she was in a car accident with her husband and two young children. For twelve minutes on the operating table, the doctors could detect no brain waves or heart activity. Elvira was clinically dead. Later, she told me that during that time she had not been completely unconscious. She clearly heard one of the doctors say 'We've lost her.' She thought to herself that she must be dead, yet she had full awareness of what was going on around her. Anyway, the main point of all this is that while they were reviving her, she had a vivid image of herself at the entrance of a long tunnel. She remembers not being afraid of walking into the tunnel. Deep in the tunnel shone a brilliant white light. As she walked, she was overcome with feelings of intense peace and joy. She wanted desperately to reach that light. Does any of this sound familiar to you?"

Ben nodded mechanically.

Stimson's lip made it painful for him to talk, and he paused for several minutes before continuing. "Suddenly, Elvira was joined in the tunnel by her father, long dead. He beseeched her to stay with them and promised her everything if she consented—unfathomable happiness, a new life. Then Elvira recognized her husband, whom she hadn't even realized was in the tunnel. He was racing toward the light, and she knew somehow that he had died in the accident."

Ben was getting impatient. "Okay, okay. But how could Elvira's hallucination about a tunnel have anything to do with Ali's fantasy?"

"Let me finish, Ben. Elvira craved that light, but innumerable conflicts held her back: duties and responsibilities to family and friends she would be turning her back on. But her obsession with the light overpowered her. She was moving toward it when the faces of her two sons flashed through her mind. They needed her, needed their mother. That brought her up short. With great effort she retraced her steps. Let me emphasize that the choice to leave the tunnel was entirely hers."

Ben leaned forward, resting his chin in his hands. He was trembling. "Are you asking me to believe that Elvira's experience was real, not a hallucination?"

"Absolutely. And in a very real sense she chose life over death. She emerged from the tunnel and felt herself floating near the ceiling of the operating room. She watched the doctors laboring to resuscitate her. She had no pain or fear, just a small lingering regret. She noticed me sitting in a lounge two floors below with three lab assistants. At that second, one of the doctors yelled, 'I've got a response.' Elvira opened her eyes, and she was home free."

Ben gripped his coffee cup. The heat from it was not sufficient to warm his shaking hands. "You're seriously arguing that Ali's cave is the same as Elvira's tunnel? And that they're real?"

"They are real, Ben. The fact that Elvira somehow knew that her husband had died, and I was in the lounge—and she identified the assistants—intrigued me. I began making inquiries. Two decades ago, few patients were revived from clinical death. But with today's effective resuscitation techniques the number of patients saved totals in the thousands. Many patients have reported experiences incredibly similar to Elvira's."

Ben focused on the row of vending machines. "You're suggesting that Ali's cave is that tunnel?" Ben asked.

"When I read descriptions of other people's experiences, there was no reason, obviously, for me to suspect they were not coincidental. But I've spent my professional life researching paranormal phenomena, and I've learned that similarities on a large scale are not just coincidence. To me, Stan's cave is a reality."

"So you've collected a few dozen similar hallucinations. That doesn't prove a damn thing."

He knew that, as Freud argued, the subconscious cannot conceive of its own demise. When confronted with imminent death, a person's mind conjures pleasant fantasies purely as an escape mechanism.

"True, I only have the stories of those people who have been revived from death, but how many millions more people have had the choice to return and turned it down?"

"We're wasting our time sitting here."

"The tapes are conclusive proof," Stimson said. "Your discovery at the cemetery corroborates the evidence. Ben, you *must* believe that Alison's experience is more than just a fantasy."

Ben started pacing again.

"Alison is trapped in the greatest conflict of her life. Love for you versus an irresistible desire for the pleasure and peace that Stan has shown her."

Avoiding Stimson's eyes, Ben asked, "How come Ali has this death wish?"

"Freud predicted, posited, that we all have it, as you know. But to get back to Elvira's case, were you aware that Stan was hit by a truck when he was eight?"

"No."

"Stan was resuscitated from clinical death," Stimson said. "He told me about it when I confronted him with the voices on the tapes. In fact, it was while he was telling me about it that he lapsed into a daze and attacked me."

A nurse entered the lounge. Ben waited until she bought coffee and left. "Do you mean that Stan *chooses* to relive his death experience? I don't believe it."

Stimson leaned back on the couch. "Yes." The throbbing in his eye and mouth flared up, a reminder of his weariness. "As with Elvira, what you and I can't imagine is the pleasure of the experience that appeals to Stan. But it is compelling."

"I should have stopped the sessions weeks ago. Or never begun them. Not with Alison as a guinea pig, anyway."

"You can't blame yourself," Stimson interrupted forcefully. "Stan's brush with death was stored in his subconscious. That recollection was rekindled by the profound trances, and the mutual hypnosis enabled him to share his experience with Alison. The hum of the telephone in the early sessions might have helped trigger Stan's memory. Its frequency is in the range of the voices in the cave."

"Why on earth would Stan share his death experience with Ali?"

"I believe Stan is very much in love with Alison. Here, she is about to marry you, and he's trying to prevent that. There, she belongs to him. Through mutual hypnosis, they shared an unusual degree of intimacy."

Ben's jealousy soared. "It's not hopeless! It can't be. There must be something we can do." His fists banged the table, his sense of defeat replaced by anger.

"Traveling through the tunnel is a joyous experience for someone who is face to face with death," Stimson said. "As Stan and Elvira were. They quickly passed, if you like, the first plateau of death. They shed the almighty ego. Alison's case is different."

"Why?"

"Alison was never in a traumatic accident of any kind. Her ego has not been abruptly shattered. Rather, she was ushered into the cave, ego partially intact. The *I* fears death more than anything else. Thanatophobia. Part of Alison's response to Stan's pleading is extreme fear, as you are well aware."

"So you're hoping that, while we sit here doing nothing, she'll save herself? That's the plan you referred to before?"

Stimson was pensive. "No. If we could somehow contact her, play on her fear of death . . ." He drifted into silence.

"You don't have a plan, do you? You're stalling. I have to get through to her. It's my only chance."

"I'm not stalling, I'm thinking aloud."

Ben shot out of the room.

"Her body temperature and pulse have dropped," Pollack said reluctantly as Ben ran to the machine. When Stimson entered, Pollack said, "One hundred over sixty-five." .

"And Stan's pressure?" Stimson asked.

"The same, I'm afraid. Their bodies are slowing in unison."

Stan's skin seemed gray. Suddenly his eyes opened and his eyeballs rolled back in his head. His pulse became dangerously erratic.

"Get breath bags and a defibrillator," Stimson ordered Pollack. "And an intern from the emergency room. Hurry." It was impossible to keep the secret any longer.

"Ali's not going to die," Ben yelled, darting toward Stan's bed. Stimson blocked his path.

"Ben!" Stimson gripped Ben's arms. "Listen

carefully. Alison will not die if you follow this procedure. If her heart stops, knead the heel of your hand into her breastbone. Press hard. The object is to squeeze her heart between her ribs and spinal column. Okay? Now pull yourself together and help me."

Ben could not help himself. He grabbed Alison's arm, fumbling frantically for her pulse.

The amplitude of Alison and Stan's brain waves had decreased. Stimson scanned the chart on the floor. Electrical activity had been diminishing steadily. Suddenly he spotted sharper waves on the graph. Quickly he picked up that section of the chart. Why hadn't Paul caught this? Stan's trace was pure theta, but Alison's contained scattered spurts of alpha waves. Stimson counted. Yes. Ten cycles a second. Was Alison resisting, trying to wake up? Or was she simply scared? Whichever, periodically she lost contact with Stan and drifted closer to wakefulness. There's a chance to save her, he almost said aloud.

"She has no pulse," Ben shouted. He beat frantically at Alison's chest.

Stan and Alison had gone into cardiac arrest. Stimson pounded Stan's chest and with his free hand pressed the Alert button over the bed. "Code Blue! Code Blue!" a voice blared over the intercom.

As Stimson worked on Stan, a plan, a wild, harebrained scheme to rescue Alison, occurred to him. It might be successful—if Alison and Stan could be revived.

# 25

A defibrillator had jolted Alison's heart to life. For a while her heart twitched with spasms, etching erratic saw-toothed waves on the oscilloscope. Injections of lidocaine finally calmed the spasms. Alison was alive, but her condition was highly unstable. She was far from being conscious.

Stan had been harder to revive. Seven five-thousand-volt shocks charged his body before the clear blips of a regular heartbeat appeared on the screen. For the next hour his respiration had to be mechanically assisted.

"George, that's insane!" Dr. Timothy Bloser's mouth gaped open. "These patients are in critical condition. Their hearts are weak, possibly damaged. You can't subject them to any unnatural stress at this point. I forbid it." Bloser's position was a commanding one, and he had the upper hand, but the case admittedly baffled him. However, Stimson's scheme was worse than asinine, it was potentially lethal.

"How long have we known each other?" Stimson asked, anxious to get back to Ben with a go-ahead from Bloser.

"Twenty-five years, give or take a few."

"Well, I'm asking you to trust an old friend and a good doctor."

"I can't do that."

"Why not?"

"For the tenth time, I have a responsibility, first of all to the patients, then to the reputation of this hospital, then to the state medical board and the AMA. There's no way I can defend or condone this kind of experimentation. What you propose is *beyond* left field, it's out of the medical ball park entirely."

Bloser, a cardiologist and the director of Clifton Hospital, was a portly, ruddy-complexioned man with little patience. Again he scanned the EEG traces. Damnedest things he'd ever seen. Impossible, in fact.

"You must let me try," Stimson demanded, his tone leaving no room for disagreement. "If you don't, their deaths will be on your conscience."

Bloser glared. "I don't recall George Stimson being so confounded stubborn. These patients are still alive, and that aside, you know damned well that it's one thing if they die of natural causes. But I can't gamble on a scheme that could easily kill them."

"But as you can see, they are dying of *unnatural* causes, and I'm fairly certain I can save them. It's *my* responsibility to try everything probable to keep them alive." Before Bloser could interrupt him, Stimson launched into yet another defense of his scheme and reiterated the facts of the case, facts that he was well aware Bloser did not entirely buy.

"No," Bloser said, "I will not grant my consent. The treatment—if you can call it that—is insanely unconventional."

"And so is this case," Stimson said.

While he argued with Bloser, Stimson's concern never drifted far from Ben. Since Alison had been resuscitated, Ben had seemed strangely restrained and sullen, keeping a silent vigil at her bedside. Stimson had administered to patients who after hours of stress lapsed into a grim, quiet mood. Usually such a mood was merely a respite before a manic explosion. Stimson prayed that Pollack had not left Ben alone in the room.

"I'm sorry, George, my decision is final."

Stimson gathered the EEG charts from Bloser's desk.

"I have only one request," Stimson said.

Bloser's eyebrows arched defensively. "What?"

"Your diagnosis. If you can give me *any* medical explanation for what is happening in that room, then I will not push my point. And keep in mind that they are dying."

Bloser watched anxiously as Stimson and Pollack set up the high-powered lamps and the generator at the foot of the beds. A thousand-watt reflector lamp with rheostat control was suspended three feet from Alison's face. Another lamp hovered over Stan. Stimson parted Alison's eyelids and inserted wire clamps to keep her eyes exposed. Her pupils were so fully dilated that her green irises were invisible. Stimson slipped earphones over Alison's head, then followed the same procedures with Stan.

Dour, Bloser stalked behind the EEG machine, annoyed at himself for relenting. Naturally he could not succeed in diagnosing this crazy case. Who the hell could? And his medical genius had been useless in preventing the patients' second cardiopulmonary arrests. Failure angered Bloser, and the fact that the encyclopedic knowledge he prided himself on meant nothing in this case goaded him.

With the lights and noise controls switched on to their lowest settings, Stimson gradually intensified the stimuli, listening for a sign of any changes from Ben and Paul.

"Anything at all?" Stimson finally asked.

"No pupil contraction," Paul answered from Stan's bedside. Ben, peering at Alison, concurred.

Stimson glanced at Bloser, then at the EEG graph. No change. Doggedly Stimson hiked the controls, bombarding Alison and Stan with maddening sensations, inputs from the real world that he hoped would swamp their minds and disrupt their communication. Their brains could not ignore such chaos as Stimson was dealing out.

"Negative," said Bloser, scrutinizing the EEG trace.

Stimson frowned. Their nervous systems must react in some way! Noise *did* thunder against their eardrums. Light *did* impinge on their retinas. Streams of electrical impulses *were* racing to their brains. Was their awareness so internally focused that they perceived none of it?

When the lamps blazed at seven hundred watts, Bloser mumbled disgruntledly, "George, this is obviously not working."

Alison's mouth opened, gasping for breath.

"Her pulse dropped," Ben said, alarmed.

"Ditto here," Pollack commented.

"Don't do it," Bloser warned. But Stimson ignored him and increased the bombardment of light and noise. The glare of the lamps off the walls was blinding. Pollack shielded his eyes.

Suddenly Ben lost Alison's pulse. His fingers dug into her wrist, searching. "Her skin is freezing," he shouted.

"Incredible!" Pollack exclaimed. "They're running away from the stimuli. Trying to escape."

Ben looked at Stimson for his denial.

"Just watch Alison for me, Ben," Stimson said soothingly. And that's when Ben exploded.

"This is a lousy plan. You're just using Ali as a guinea pig for your own purpose. So you can add another monograph to your collection."

"Ben," Pollack shouted, "don't say anything you're only going to regret. Stimson is trying to save Alison."

"Like hell. He's just improvising as he goes along. And handing out a lot of doubletalk."

"God damn it, Ben, not now." Pollack advanced toward Ben. "We're in the middle of a crisis, for God's sake. So shut up and help us."

As quickly as it had come, Ben's choler dissipated. Confused and close to tears again, he shrugged halfheartedly and fumbled for Alison's wrist. He barely felt a pulse.

Stimson threw the switch setting the lights rapidly flashing. The flicker was more unbearable than the steady glare. If Alison broke sync for even a second, the bombardment might register with her, driving a wedge between her mind and Stan's.

Alison's face contorted.

"Stop it!" Ben screamed. "You're torturing her."

"That's not pain," Stimson said. "It's fear."

At that moment Bloser spotted the change. Alison's brainwave pattern had slowed to the alpha waves of light sleep. "Alpha!" he blurted.

Elated, Stimson increased the bombardment even more. Explosions of blinding light ricocheted off the walls. Pollack shut his eyes, but he could still detect the flashes.

"You're going to blind them," Bloser yelled, turning his back to the beds.

Stimson gambled, hiking the lights, then upping the noise to one hundred and thirty decibels, though he realized that in thirty seconds permanent ear damage could result.

Stan's piercing voice filled the room. "Leeeavv-veeeusalllooone."

Bloser was flabbergasted, but before he could respond, Ben said excitedly, "Alison's pupils are contracting."

Stimson counted the seconds, trying to keep cool. If he had to, he would risk impairing Alison's hearing.

"Damn," Bloser said. "Her theta's returning." Seconds later he added, "Her brain waves are not in sync with Stan's."

"Damn it," Pollack said, rushing to the EEG machine. "She just can't pull free of Stan."

Stimson's eyes widened. "That's it! *Can't pull free.* That's it! Paul, you put your finger on it!"

"What are you talking about?" Pollack asked.

"I have to chance it." In a split second Stimson had switched off Stan's lamp and yanked the plug connecting Stan's headphones to the noise generator. "Why didn't I think of this before?"

The sudden plunge in light intensity jarred everyone.

"What the hell are you doing?" Ben yelled.

But his question was drowned out by Bloser's booming voice. "She's producing beta waves!" His excitement surprised him. The waves were sporadic and feeble at first, but soon their number and amplitude sprawled across the graph. "Alison is regaining consciousness!"

In calculated increments, Stimson diminished the light and noise.

Everyone stared at Alison except Stimson, who gazed blankly at the control panel, afraid to look at Stan. Stan had been tethered to the real world by a thin rubber band. By pulling the plugs, Stimson had, in effect, snapped that rubber band and propelled Stan away from Alison—and farther from reality. Stimson had saved Alison, but at what cost to Stan?

# 26

For the remainder of the day, Stan lay comatose in
the Intensive Care Unit. Dr. Bloser, concerned by
Stan's shallow, erratic breathing, put him in an
oxygen tent. Paradoxically, while Stan's life signs
grew progressively weaker, his brain surged with
activity. "It's as though Stan were frantically
attempting to contact Alison," Pollack commented.

Nina arrived shortly after Pollack phoned her.
Stan's condition, and Pollack's explanation of the
events leading up to it, left her sitting by Stan's bed,
numb and confused.

Alison awakened around noon and was shifted at
Ben's urging to a private room. He'd also nagged

Pollack and Stimson to stop hanging around and get some rest and they left. Alison recognized Ben immediately and responded to his questions, but her speech was halting, as she was not fully cognizant. Her dilated pupils, slow reflexes, and frequent memory lapses suggested to Ben that she was still somehow tuned in to Stan's blandishments. Before leaving, Stimson had run EEG tests on Alison and had determined that sporadic low-level theta waves were responsible for her foggy awareness. He had to agree with Ben that the telepathic bond between Alison and Stan had been weakened but not broken.

Nevertheless, Stimson's success in itself offered Ben a modicum of hope, and he seized it. Relentlessly he labored to engage Alison in conversation, fighting to focus her consciousness on him, on their wedding, on their future together. But by ten o'clock that night, his voice hoarse, his throat burning, Ben had done little to lift Alison's haze. At Dr. Bloser's insistence, Ben permitted Alison to sleep.

The next morning Bloser found Ben red-eyed and haggard, slumped on the chair beside Alison's bed. She still slept.

"Today's March fifteenth," Ben said.

"So?"

"Nothing."

"What kind of night did she have?" Dr. Bloser asked, feeling Alison's forehead.

"Rotten," Ben answered despondently. "For long periods she tossed and mumbled in her sleep." He had not succeeded in deciphering Alison's groans, and he did not tell Bloser that he believed her restless periods corresponded to Stan's efforts to reestablish domination over her. The day before, Bloser had made it emphatically clear that he wouldn't tolerate any more talk about "that telepathy nonsense."

"Go home and rest. Keep George company. Anything, but get out of here," Dr. Bloser advised curtly as he took Alison's pulse. He was irritable. He regretted having started his rounds by checking in on Stan. This damn case had him stymied. For some inexplicable reason, Fredericks's condition had deteriorated to the point that his vital functions were now fully maintained by a heart-and-lung machine. More bewildering still were the recent EEG traces. The confounded patterns! The left side of his brain was virtually inactive, almost displaying the flat curve characteristic of death. But the right hemisphere, which governs perception and spatial orientation, pulsed wildly with currents. The night intern, who had recorded the traces, was dumbfounded by them.

"Dr. Bloser," he had asked, "what can this fellow possibly be perceiving?"

"Nothing," Bloser retorted.

Despite Bloser's unpleasant manner, Ben remained by Alison's side. He wanted to be near when she awoke and had no intention of leaving her alone. She woke up at about ten o'clock, but to Ben's dismay she was no more lucid than she had been the previous day. After several hours of testing, Bloser concluded that physically, at least, Alison was fit. Her vital signs were strong. Her heart had not been damaged. On this evidence and with Stimson's approval, Ben insisted on taking her home, happy to get her out of the hospital and farther away from Stan. Familiar surroundings, he reasoned, might help tighten her grip on the real world and wrench her from Stan's influence.

But her progress in that regard as the day wore on was not encouraging. Except for an occasional comment or smile at Stimson, she remained bemused, preoccupied, not all there.

Ben glowered at the kitchen clock. It was eight-thirty. Alison had been asleep for an hour. March 16 would soon dawn, and the thought made Ben queasy.

"We've got to awaken her," Ben snapped, interrupting Stimson's speculation on Alison's mental state. After dinner, when Alison had excused herself and gone to bed, he and Stimson had argued about how to sever the tie still binding Alison and Stan.

"You keep forcing her to talk about wedding plans," Stimson said, "and it's not helping. In fact, she seemed to me to be increasingly resistant about discussing that topic."

Ben fumed. "Then we have to take Stan off the respirator. He has to die before Alison can resume a normal life with me. I'll take the responsibility of pulling the plug myself." The issue of Stan's death had become an obsession with him.

Stimson patted him on the shoulder. "If you could hear yourself, you'd be appalled by what you're suggesting. It's not a matter of responsibility, it's a matter of ethics, plain and simple. As long as Stan exhibits brain-wave activity, every effort must be made to sustain his bodily functions." Stimson leaned against the kitchen counter, his hands supporting his weary head. At length he sighed, "Stan's brain, or part of it anyway, is very much alive."

Ben couldn't contain himself. "Stan is trying to dominate Ali! You, Pollack and I all recognize that fact. By keeping Stan alive, we're increasing the probability that he will succeed."

"We're not *keeping* Stan alive, Ben. By medical definition he *is* alive."

Ben implored Stimson. "You've admitted that Stan's death wish is so strong that it's highly unlikely we can save him. Well, Christ! Think of Ali!"

"I am," Stimson said. "If Stan loses all brain activity, it would apparently indicate that he's chosen to die. You know very well, Ben, that we cannot play God and make that decision for him."

"But Alison's life could be needlessly taken from her. And we're in a position to do something about it."

"Look at it this way," Stimson said, grasping for an argument that would make sense to Ben. "If we were to terminate Stan's life before his control over Alison is completely eroded, what are the consequences for Alison? I hate to imagine what they would be, how screwed up her life could be."

Ben hesitated. He hadn't considered the possibility that Stan's premature death might affect Alison. "There would be no consequences," he shot back defensively.

"Are you positive?" Stimson asked. "Are you so sure that Alison herself might not also die? Or, if she lived, that she would not be psychotic for the rest of her life?"

Ben sank into a chair. The situation now seemed hopeless. He envisioned two tombstones with the date March 16 chiseled on their surfaces. "We have to take that chance," he said. "It's our only option."

"No," Stimson replied. "I'm convinced that we can make headway if we play on Alison's fear of death. Once she begins to respond to that tack, we can then convince her that she has a whole happy life in front of her." Stimson noticed that Ben was listening and not arguing for a change, so he hurried on. "It's the reverse of the Tibetan *Book of the Dead*."

"What?"

"The Tibetan *Book of the Dead*. It's an eighth-century text—"

"I know what it is," Ben barked. "What's the connection with Alison?"

"It's supposed to be read to a dying person to ease the fear and trauma of death. Among other things, it stresses that loved ones must persuade the departing soul that his or her purpose on earth has been fulfilled and that those left behind will not mourn. In other words, the living emotionally release the dying. You must do just the opposite with Alison. In effect, invert every statement in the Tibetan manual to make dying emotionally impossible for her. What it all adds up to, Ben, is that Alison is the only person who can destroy the link with Stan."

Ben was exasperated. "How in the hell do I get her to concentrate on all that stuff when I can barely communicate with her? She's hardly listening to me. You even think she's resisting me."

"That's what I'm trying to figure out. Perhaps

with the aid of drugs, but that's off the top of my head." Stimson grew introspective.

Ben leaped from the chair. "I have the answer! I'm not communicating with Alison because she and I are just not on the same wavelength. We have no substantial rapport. However, in a mutual trance we would!"

Stimson's face was ashen. "My God, Ben, do you realize the danger in what you're proposing?"

Ben's mind raced. "The bond between Ali and Stan was forged at a subliminal level. So it's reasonable that it can be cut only at that depth. Don't you see? I have to adjust to Ali's level of reality in order to convince her to save herself and to dissociate herself from Stan."

"Even so, it's much too risky."

"Then how else can I heighten her fear of death—which you're certain is the key? Name one way besides mutual hypnosis in which my pleading with her would be more effective."

"Ben, one part of Alison is afraid to die, but another part has glimpsed a totally different existence, evidently a joyous, infinitely peaceful one, from all accounts. Persuasion can work both ways."

"Never!"

"But look at Stan's amazing influence on Alison."

"I don't have Alison's problems. There's simply no way that I'll fall under that kind of spell."

"But—"

"Don't forget, I'm talking about one session, only one session. Nothing Alison says in one session can establish control over my mind. Will you conduct the session?"

"Ben, I'm worried. Stan led Alison into the cave. And I'd bet that for the first few times she had no idea that she was confronting her own death."

"So?"

"You'd be entering the cave by your own free will. That might be something like the equivalent of suicide. There are religious admonitions—"

"Bullshit!"

Stimson pursued what he knew was a losing battle, and in the end he confessed that he had no alternative plan for separating Alison's subconscious from Stan's.

"Well, will you conduct the session or not?"

Stimson was pensive. "If you haven't been able to get Alison to concentrate in the last two days, how do you expect to hypnotize her?"

"I'll try. That's the best I can do. But I have to make the attempt.

Stimson went into the dining room. From the third drawer of the breakfront, beneath the table linens, he removed the ashtray he had hidden there after observing Alison's fixation with it.

Ben stood in the doorway. "What in the world are you doing?"

"We'll prepare this session very carefully," Stimson said, handing the ashtray to Ben. "You might need this to hypnotize Alison. Now you must be ready for all contingencies."

# 27

Stimson could only hope that Ben's solution wouldn't backfire. Sighing, he began elaborating on the similarities between dying as described in the Tibetan text and as related by individuals resuscitated from clinical death—the tunnel and brilliant light, the sensation of cosmic unity, the voices and visions of spirits. "The Tibetans teach that these elements characterize death for all people," Stimson concluded, "but that a person who has lived a spiritual life experiences them with much less fear."

Ultimately, Ben balked at the religious notions of the tunnel serving as a passageway to the hereafter and of the light representing a universal God. For him, the death imagery was strictly psychological, a defensive fantasy created by the subconscious, which could not conceive of its own demise. The fantasy had a subjective reality, not an objective one. As he and Stimson bandied these arguments back and forth, Ben kept checking his watch. Time was wasting, and he needed Stimson's help.

Stimson finally hypnotized Ben, implanting the posthypnotic suggestion that would permit him to wake Ben from the mutual trance. Then he awakened Ben, and together they went upstairs. It was ten-thirty when Ben nervously entered the bedroom trailed by Stimson.

Alison must have been sleeping lightly, for she awoke briefly when Ben slid a chair next to the bed and sat down.

"Ali, please don't go back to sleep," Ben said, rising to sit on the bed.

She gazed blankly at him. He pulled her forward, jostling her. "Honey, you can sleep later."

Her eyelids drooped; her body was pliant. She had seemed more alert when she'd come home from the hospital. Ben's coaxing failed to arouse her. He opened the window to circulate cold air in the room. "You'll feel stronger if you get up and walk," he said, as Alison snuggled under the blanket. He threw back the covers and started to drag her to her feet when Stimson interrupted him, taking Alison's hand.

"Let me help you," he said. "Do you recognize me?"

"Yes. I feel woozy."

"You'll feel much better after a little exercise." Stimson eased Alison to her feet. Ben suppressed his injured pride. The important thing was that Stimson had Alison up and around.

After walking her in the hall, Stimson brought her back to the bedroom and stopped by the window. "What a bright night!" Stimson exclaimed, hoping some of his exuberance would rub off on her. He suggested she inhale deeply, and as she breathed the cold air, her body shuddered.

Good, Ben noted, she's reacting to stimuli. He shut the window.

"Let's go downstairs for a short jaunt," Stimson said.

"Must we?" Her voice sounded weak.

"I'd like you to. We'd be more comfortable in the living room. And it's warmer there. Ben has a cozy fire blazing."

"Okay." She shrugged.

Stimson led her to Ben. "Ben will take you downstairs." As Ben held out his hand, she withdrew behind Stimson. "Alison, Ben wants to help you, too." She would not budge. Gently he nudged her toward Ben, and only because of his persistence did she allow Ben to assist her.

Descending the staircase, Ben worked hard to win Alison's attention, well aware that the more readily she related to him, the greater his chance of creating a successful mutual trance.

When Alison had settled on the sofa, Ben placed a chair in front of her. "Ali, are you comfortable?"

She did not answer, avoiding his eyes. He was tempted to ask her why she was fighting him but decided against it. He doubted if she'd even understand what he meant.

Stimson talked animatedly to Alison while Ben

fetched the ashtray from the dining room. For the first time, he wondered what he was about to experience under mutual hypnosis and how he'd react. Lifting the ashtray from the table, his hands trembled. Everything depended on the effectiveness of the plan.

Alison immediately focused on the ashtray. Stimson sat in front of her, ready to begin the session.

"We decided that I would hypnotize her," Ben protested when Stimson made no move to get up.

Stimson reached for the ashtray. He intended to try and enter a mutual trance with Alison himself.

Ben backed away. "I got her into this mess, and I'll get her out."

"Ben, this session is important. I'll hypnotize Alison."

"No. This is insane!"

"It's the only way, Ben. If you try to hypnotize her, she's likely to resist you, as she has since she came home. Give me the ashtray, she's drifting fast."

Alison's stare was riveted to the ashtray, her eyes watery, her mouth slightly parted. They both realized at once that there would be no need to hypnotize her, she had automatically plunged into a deep trance.

"The ashtray," Stimson requested. "I'm going to have her hypnotize me."

"You're crazy!" yelled Ben. "I haven't given you a posthypnotic suggestion. How would I wake you?"

"I'd eventually fall asleep and awaken naturally," Stimson answered. "It's much safer for me than for you, Ben. You're almost hysterical now, and I doubt that you can control the situation if Alison hypnotized you."

"Get up!" Ben yelled. "We're losing precious time arguing." He grabbed Stimson's arm and yanked him from the chair. Ben sat down and began swinging the ashtray wildly past Alison's face.

"For God's sake, Ben, get a hold on yourself," said Stimson, rubbing his arm. He grasped Ben's wrist and slowed the ashtray to a circular movement. "Do it this way."

"Ali, it's Ben. I understand what you're going through. The excitement and the fear. Listen to my voice. It will comfort you. Ali, I want to share your experience with you. Guide me through the cave. Show me the bright light and the flowers. What I'm requesting may be difficult, but you *will* do it for me. Help me enter the cave."

Her shoulders slouched as her glassy eyes tracked the path of the ashtray.

"Please, Ali. I'm begging you. Take me with you."

No response. Ben worried that she had already traveled too deeply into the cave to hear him.

"Ali, don't leave without me." He continued pleading, anxious that she had guessed his real intention.

Suddenly Alison began describing the cave in a mesmerizing voice. Ben fixed his gaze on her eyes and paced his breathing to relax himself. He had no problem concentrating on her words, and he soon felt lightheaded. The room seemed cold, despite the fire, and he shivered.

He had been hypnotized many times before, but the present experience was uncomfortably different. Alison's chilled breath numbed his face; his vision blurred. His arms and legs felt as if they'd been shot full of Novocain. The difference, he supposed, was due to the fact that he was desperate to be hypnotized, and that urgency was somehow intensifying his experience.

Ben quickly realized that Alison's voice possessed a strange pitch that seemed to resonate in the center of his head. Had Stimson noticed it? It was a primitive, intoxicating sound. In his blurred vision, Alison's face shimmered and grew transparent like a building that vanishes in the heat waves of a summer day.

"Eeeeeeeeeeeeeeeeeeeeeeeeee!"

The shrill yell startled him, echoing in his ears, then fading. Relax, damn it, he warned himself. You're too tense. The secret is to let go.

"Eeeeeeeeeeeeeeeeeeeeeeeee!"

Christ, what's that? he thought. Again the shriek, this time accompanied by a dazzling flash of white light. Instinctively he tried to blink but couldn't. His eyelids were frozen open. Fear seized him. He attempted to glance at Stimson, but his body seemed paralyzed. A blistering light filled his vision.

"Beeeeeee! Beeeeeee!"

The sound knifed into his eardrums, and he cringed in pain and panic. Everything went black.

*"Ben. Ben. I'm right here."*

*Alison floated just in front of him, calling his name. He reached out to embrace her, but his hands passed through her. The same thing happened when he attempted to touch himself. Nothing in.the cave was tangible, yet everything seemed uncannily real. Was he now pure conscience? Pure mind?*

*Alison drifted closer. He could see her and also see through her. There was an eerie tranquillity in the cave's vacuous silence, an uncanny sense of belonging. Yet instinctively he knew that to venture a step farther meant certain death.*

*"You must relax, Ben. Don't be afraid."*

*But he was terrified.*

*"Ben, follow me."*

*No! he wanted to shout. Ali, come back with me! But his fear rendered him speechless. Was this the reason Ali had been almost helpless against Stan's coaxing? The paralysis of fear? Or did she genuinely not want to die?*

*"Ben, I've nearly conquered the fear. Eventually you can, too."*

*He must get a grip on himself so he could persuade her to awaken when he did. She was still afraid, so he had a chance, probably his last chance.*

*Alison drifted away from him and beckoned. "Hurry," she said.*

*He couldn't move. What did Alison find so appealing about the cave? About the death experience? He felt no joy or peace, glimpsed no unearthly splendor. Then he remembered Stimson's observations: Entering the cave by your own free will must be like dying by suicide.*

*"Hurry, Ben," Alison said.*

*"No! She wanted him to die! Without touching him, she was drawing him deeper into the cave and toward the light. Panic convulsed him. He did not want to die. Far ahead he spotted Stan surrounded by people.*

*"Join us, Ben," Alison whispered. "Your suffering will only be temporary."*

**"NO! I DON'T WANT TO DIE!"**

"I don't want to die, Alison, come back with me!"

Ben's shouts increased Stimson's frantic attempts to wake him up.

"You *will* obey me," Stimson demanded. Sweat ran down his face. He wasn't getting through to Ben. The ashtray fell from Ben's hands and crashed to the floor. Ben toppled off the chair. Immediately Stimson knelt beside him. Ben's eyes opened. Stimson twisted Ben's head, but his eyeballs did not roll. He had no reflexes, no pulse.

Then Alison slumped on the sofa, her skin gray. She had stopped breathing.

Stimson raced to the hall phone and summoned an ambulance. Before it arrived he might be able to revive Ben or Alison, but not both of them at the same time.

# 28

Ben was aware of his nostrils pinched closed, pressure against his mouth, air being painfully forced into his lungs. Otherwise, the rest of his body felt unresponsive, dead. He tried but could not move his arms or legs.

He opened his eyes. A blurred object close to his face obstructed his vision, then he recognized Stimson's face inches away. Stimson's lips were tight against his own, administering mouth-to-mouth resuscitation. Ben rolled his eyes and scanned the ceiling. He noticed a slight crack in the corner above his head. Hazily, his mind began working again. He was alive! He had made it out of the cave! Or had Stimson saved him? Who cared, he was alive!

A high-pitched sound, coming closer, louder, rang in his ears. For a second he thought it was a voice from the cave. Ali's? His heart skipped a beat, but no, he could move his fingers, he was alive. The noise, he soon realized, was a siren, a police or ambulance siren. Yes, an ambulance. For him? For Ali?

Where was Ali? he wondered. He yearned to know. He distinctly remembered that she had stayed behind to help him overcome his fear. She had been so concerned over his fright and reluctance. She wanted him to join her. Then his mind drew a blank. Everything had gone black until he felt Stimson's breath filling his lungs. Had Ali left the cave, too? Returned to life? Ali had tried to take his life! A wave of terror shot through him.

The siren wailed outside the house.

From his prone position on the floor, Ben strained to turn his head toward the sofa, but his body was paralyzed with fear. He moved his eyes, searching for Alison, but glimpsed only the frayed side of the sofa, the arm eclipsing his view.

Stimson peered at him. "Ben, can you talk?"

The siren stopped. The ambulance had arrived. "Ben, can you hear me?"

He blinked frantically, sick that this was his only means of communication. He wanted to say so much: How is Ali? Where is she? She tried to kill me!

The doorbell chimed.

"If you can hear me," Stimson said, standing, "I'll be right back. Don't worry, help is here."

Stimson disappeared, and Ben heard muffled

voices at the door. Two men in white uniforms quickly laid a stretcher beside him. Two more attendants hurried to the sofa, but Ben could not see what they were doing.

They lifted him onto the stretcher, and he struggled to twist his neck to see Alison, but it was useless.

"Take it easy lifting her," he heard Stimson say.

In the hall, Ben glimpsed the wall clock. It was after midnight. March 16 had begun! He blinked wildly with the fear that Alison would die today and take him with her.

"What is it, Ben?" Stimson was beside him. "Are you in pain?"

I'm numb, traumatized, he blinked. You've got to understand. Ali's overcome her fear of the cave. She tried to coax me deeper into the cave. I'm concerned about her, but I fear for my own safety. If Ali's still in the cave, she might still be able to influence me.

"We'll do something to alleviate the pain just as soon as we get you in the ambulance." Stimson patted Ben's arm.

Ben glanced at the clock again, and Stimson followed his gaze. He understood, but there was nothing he could say.

Abruptly a black mask was cupped over Ben's mouth and nose and surging oxygen burned his lungs. He was carried into the ambulance, his stretcher placed against a rack on the wall. Ali's stretcher was placed on the opposite wall. She was only a few feet from him, but he couldn't see her. He didn't sense her tugging influence, yet he felt dangerously vulnerable. He knew that he would not be completely safe until the next twenty-four hours had passed.

One of the attendants filled a hypodermic syringe and bent over Alison. He was giving her an injection. Thank God, Ben sighed. She must be alive. Or did it mean that she had not awakened? That she was in the cave trying to reach him?

The ambulance screeched forward, speeding, its siren screaming in the night.

# 29

Stimson sat by Ben's bed, puzzled by his paralysis. He had begun mouth-to-mouth resuscitation immediately after phoning for the ambulance, so Ben could not possibly have suffered any brain damage. Severe shock could account for the paralysis and muteness. Considering his shouting, coming out of the trance, Stimson had to assume that Ben was traumatized by whatever he had seen or heard in the cave.

Devising a code whereby Ben blinked once for yes and twice for no, Stimson quickly learned that Ben was not in pain and that he was anxious about Alison.

"Ben, I'm going to level with you. Alison is alive. And she's breathing on her own. But I'd be a fool not to tell you that she hasn't awakened, and her prognosis is uncertain." He held Ben's hand. "At the moment, you must think of yourself. Your symptoms are no doubt the result of shock, which means they should soon disappear."

Ben closed his eyes. The night had been hell. While a team of doctors had worked to revive Alison, Ben had fought hard to suppress the cave imagery that periodically flooded his mind. He could not be sure whether the visions were vivid memories of his experience or fresh glimpses into the cave, and that troubled him. Whichever, he instinctively knew that he had to overpower the hallucinations, for they were the links between him and the cave, him and death. He began multiplying large numbers in his head to focus on analytical things and to shake his mind free of the hallucinations.

His eyes never wandered far from the wall clock in his hospital room. He couldn't wait until the sixteenth was over.

Stimson brought reports of Alison and Stan's condition. Alison seemed to be gaining strength, but Stan's brain activity was steadily diminishing. Nina came in several times, her eyes red from crying. Even if he could have talked, Ben wouldn't have known what to say to her.

Around three in the afternoon, Pollack appeared. He had come from the Intensive Care Unit to announce that Stan's EEG trace was getting weaker. For the first time since the hypnosis, Ben felt himself relaxing, but he refused to let himself relax too much and started in on multiplication tables.

At seven-thirty that evening, Stimson was paged. When he returned to Ben's room, he said, "Stan has just died." He sat at the foot of Ben's bed. *"Stan is dead, and Alison is alive.* Do you understand what that means? Alison has just made it over the biggest hurdle. She must have an incredible will to live."

An hour later Ben began to recover. He was sitting up. His voice returned. The only remnant of the paralysis was a weakness in his legs. Dr. Bloser and Pollack dropped in as Ben shuffled around the room. When they left, his words burst out in a breathless, horrified voice. Stimson had him sit down and start again. He explained exactly what had happened during the trance.

"Ali didn't want me to come back. She tried to lead me deeper into the cave, to stay with her. She said she was overcoming her fear of death and was happy. That I'd be, too. She wants me to die with her, to—"

"Calm down," Stimson interrupted. "Whatever happened in the cave is over and done with. You are out of the cave and very much alive. Alison is alive."

"You don't understand. Ali wants me with her *there,* not here."

"Ben, you're overreacting to the trance, awful as it was. Stan has died, and Alison did not choose to go with him."

"Alison might die before midnight and try to take me with her." He glanced at the clock. The day would end in less than three hours. Stimson grabbed Ben's arm. "Ben, that's past. You're alive. Whatever influence Alison tried to exert over you in the cave is over. You have nothing to fear from her now. She's obviously made her decision."

"Let's go see her. I feel up to it."

Stimson found a wheelchair and pushed Ben to Alison's room.

Alison lay on her side, curled in a fetal position, her skin wan. He and Alison were alive! That was proof she had chosen life over death, him over Stan. Ben looked at Stimson and, for the first time in days, smiled. He gazed at her for a long time. At length he asked, "Why hasn't she awakened yet?"

"I can't figure it out, Ben, but I have great faith that she will. As I mentioned to you, her metabolism during the trance was so slow that, for the short time she was without oxygen, there was miraculously little if any damage. Her health is fine."

"That was an awful choice you had to make. I've been so preoccupied with Alison and myself ever since you arrived that I've been terribly inconsiderate and never so much as thanked you—"

"The important thing is that you and Alison are both alive." Stimson hid his blushing face by stooping over to check Alison's chart at the end of her bed.

At midnight, Stimson and Ben were still in Alison's room. Ben was truly astonished that he was still alive.

"Well, the worst is over," Stimson said, then grinned. "It's March seventeenth."

"Thank God." Ben stretched and allowed himself to relax completely. "Still, I'll feel better when Alison wakes up. This sounds silly, but all day I've been doing math calculations in my head whenever I started remembering the cave experience. It was the only way I could divert my thoughts."

"You were frightened, understandably so."

"Why don't you go back to my room and get some sleep? You look beat. I'm all right now." He had an overwhelming urge to be alone with Alison.

"Let me wheel you to your room."

Ben stood and walked to assure Stimson that he was all right. "I'm going to stay here. I want Ali to see me as soon as she wakes up."

"All right, then. I'll be down the hall if you want me."

The silence of the room was broken by Alison's rhythmic breathing. Ben counted; her respiration rate was normal. He held his hand near her face; her breath was warm. Taking her pulse, he noticed that her skin seemed cold, but he concluded that that was faulty, emotional judgment on his part. Her body was functioning normally. But why hadn't she awakened? Was she fighting for her life? Ben wondered. Was there brain damage they hadn't detected? Was she this minute fighting the attraction of the cave and trying to anchor herself in reality, as Ben had had to do? Ben was consumed with guilt for what he had done to her. For the purpose of his own damn project. For money and fame and all the trappings that wouldn't mean a damn thing without Alison.

"Oh, God," he whispered, "let her wake up. Give me a chance to make it up to her."

Struck with the possibility that Alison might be able to hear him, he leaned close to her. The familiar smell of her hair rekindled memories of the life they had shared together before he had inflicted this nightmare on her.

"Ali, if you can hear me, I love you. Please believe that I want you back more than anything else in this world. I know you feel the same way." He outlined the contours of her face with his finger. "Ali, you've got to wake up. I forgive you for trying to persuade me to stay in the cave with you, and you must forgive me for being so greedy, for risking our happiness together. I swear I'll make it up to you. We can start over again. Please wake up."

Alison did not stir. Depressed, Ben realized how miserably he had failed in the cave, how cowardly his behavior had been. Had he conquered his fear, he would have been able to convince Alison to awaken when he did. She'd be well now, and this agonizing waiting would be over. Suddenly an idea struck him. Perhaps what Alison needed now more than ever to help her come out of the trance was persuasion. Maybe she couldn't wake up on her own. Stimson, after all, had helped pull him from the cave.

Gently, Ben gripped Alison's shoulders. "Ali, you *can* hear me. *You must wake up. You must.* Concentrate on my words. My voice. If you try hard enough you can do it. Let me help you."

He listened for some change in her respiration, any sound that would indicate she had heard him. The threat of losing Alison brought tears to his eyes. He couldn't bear losing her. He slipped an arm underneath her and hugged her. He recalled their plans for the wedding and how carefree their lives had been until he talked himself out. Dejected and drained, he decided to sleep for a few hours. He asked the nurse on night duty at the desk to wake him the second Alison opened her eyes.

The dimly lit hall was tinged red by the fuzzy light of the Exit signs. He passed closed doors, some with Do Not Disturb signs, and an empty reception area. He turned down the deserted corridor that led to his room. The silence was awful. It seemed both to amplify his guilt and to intensify his love for Alison. Passing the second doorway, his legs suddenly felt weak, and he leaned against the wall for support. He should have let Stimson help him to his room, he was not as strong as he thought. He considered yelling for an attendant, but that would awaken the other patients. Anyway, he was close to his room. Squinting to read the room number on the opposite door, he realized that his vision was blurring. The numbers zoomed in and out of focus. His head throbbed, and the wall beneath his fingers felt like a slab of ice. No! The wall wasn't cold. The chill came from his hands. And now his feet were cold. His entire body was freezing. Immediately he recognized what was happening to him. He had dropped his defenses. Frantically he shook his head to shrug off the cave imagery that was rapidly absorbing his concentration. But it persisted. He tried to scream for help, but his throat seemed numb. He mustn't panic. Wasn't this the opportunity he'd been praying for? A chance to make contact with Alison. To save her. In order to calm himself he breathed deeply. He would not fail again.

Coooommmmmeeeee. Cccccooooommmm-meeeee. Cccooommmeee. The shrill sound pierced his ears. Sliding down the wall, he saw an apparition drifting toward him. Alison beckoned him to follow her. "No, Ali, you must come back with me!" He could speak! That amazed him. His shout reverberated in the hall.

In Ben's room, Stimson sat up with a start.

*Blackness. Then he was in the cave, squinting in its glare, searching for Ali. The cave's vacuous silence frightened him, but he was determined to master his emotions.*

"Beeeeeeeen! Beeeeeeeeeeen!"

*He turned at the sound of the echo. Through the inky blackness that surrounded the tunnel's exit he could see Stimson running down the hospital corridor. It was like looking through the back end of a telescope, everything small and remote, Stimson's voice a shrill echo.*

"Ben, you've come back."

*Abruptly he turned. Ali's transparent image stood in front of him, shimmering.*

"Ben, don't leave again. Please. Stay here with me."

*His throat felt constricted, but he forced himself to speak.* "Ali, why here? Come back with me. We have a whole life to live together."

"I have no problems here, Ben."

"Come back, Ali, and I promise we'll work out your problems together. We can do it."

"Beeeeen yoooooouuuu muuuust waaaakeeee uuuup! Liisteeen toooo meeee!"

*He glimpsed Stimson kneeling beside his own body, frantically shaking it. Funny, he felt nothing except the eerie sensation of being out of his body, observing it from afar. Ali was smiling.*

"Don't listen to Stimson, Ben. Stay with me."

*He spoke firmly and lovingly. "Ali, I'm not going to die. I'm going to return. The only way I'll ever have peace of mind is if you come with me. You must do it for me. For us."*

*The people gathering in the distance, beckoning Alison, did not scare him. He would not fail this time. He alone held her undivided attention.*

*"Ben, I love you," she said, but she came no closer to him.*

*Instinctively he sensed that he could not go deeper into the cave and still possess the willpower to return. Ali would have to come to him. He offered her his hand.*

*"Ali, please," he begged. Through her body he could see the brilliant light at the other end of the tunnel. With his fear partly conquered, the light seemed to exert a magnetic pull on him and he diverted his gaze. Stimson's hollow cries were a comfort. A bridge back to the real world.*

*He had to turn his back on the light, its pull was becoming so strong. Ali stood behind him.*

*"Ali, you can return if you want to. All it takes is a strong enough desire. Focus your attention on Stimson and the others. Look at them. Listen to their voices. They can anchor you."*

*Stimson and two attendants were lifting his body onto a stretcher. He knew he could not stay in the cave much longer; there was something uncannily compelling about it.*

*"Ali," he pleaded, "I've got to go back now. If you really love me as much as you say you do, then follow me. Don't make me suffer by having to live without you. Please."*

*The light pulled stronger.*

With one hand extended behind him, reaching out for Ali, he began drifting toward the black mist. Stimson's voice became more solid; the image of his own body was growing in size.

He knew that he could not look back at the light. That would spell inevitable death. He could only pray that if Ali loved him enough she was already following him out of the cave.

Mist was beginning to race into his nostrils and ears and into his mouth so that when he tried to call to Alison no words came out. It was getting harder to propel himself forward.

He felt a hand brush through his. He wanted to turn around, to say something encouraging to Ali, but didn't dare. He groped behind his back for the hand, felt it again, then hurtled himself into the blackness.

# 30

Solemnly Ben bowed his head as Stan's casket was lowered into the ground. The morning downpour had changed to a sporadic drizzle. A strong wind tugged at his umbrella. He held Alison close to him, held her so tightly he'd almost lost sensation in his arm. He was overjoyed at having her back and couldn't stop himself from hugging her. In the little time they'd had together since awakening, he'd even pressed her into setting a wedding date: three weeks from Sunday. He was determined not to lose her.

Father O'Rouke sprinkled holy water over the descending casket and intoned, "O Cor Jesu, rogo te, ne permittas mori me." Stimson crossed himself.

Pollack continued to stare blankly at his shoes as he had done throughout the service.

"Ben, I want to go over to Nina."

"Honey, we'll both go when the service is over. Her parents are strong support." He raised her coat collar against the biting wind.

He had not wanted Alison at Stan's funeral, but all his arguments to keep her home had failed. Physically, she was strong. And Stan's death seemed to have released her from her amnesia, for she remembered everything that had taken place in the cave. Those memories, and her sense of responsibility to Nina, were the grounds on which he had finally let Alison attend the service.

Now he was sorry he had given in. Since they had arrived at the cemetery he felt certain he had detected a change in her mood. She had become sullen and introspective. She closed her eyes and rested her head against his shoulder and Ben asked, "Ali, are you sure you wouldn't be more comfortable in the car?"

"No, Ben. I want to stay here."

The rain let up briefly and he tilted his umbrella to cut off Alison's line of sight to the open grave that had been dug a few feet away from Stan's. In the chaos of the last day, no one had thought to call the cemetery to say that there would be only one burial. Sight of what was to have been Alison's grave had hit Ben hard; the gaping hole filled him with dread. In his peripheral vision he watched Alison. She appeared to be silently praying. She knew the grave had been meant for her, and she seemed to accept its presence with a calm that deeply disturbed Ben. He was fearful that sight of the grave might trigger a return of her death wish. Could something as potent as what she had experienced, he wondered, just vanish?

Ceremoniously, Father O'Rouke tossed a shovel of mud onto the casket and uttered, "Domine, exaudi orationem meam. Et clamor meus ad te veniat." As the prayers ended, the crowd headed toward their cars. Alison and Ben walked over to Nina. Ben could barely bring himself to look at her as she and Alison embraced. At the sound of her sobbing, he touched her arm and looked quickly away. Stimson was about to get into Pollack's station wagon to go to the airport and Ben excused himself to join Stimson.

"Again," said Ben, "I have to thank you for everything you've done. For me and for Ali."

"Ben, we all did what we could. Don't be too hard on yourself over Stan's death. It will do no good."

Ben held fast to Stimson's handshake. "You don't think Ali regrets having come back?"

From inside the car Pollack yelled, "We better hurry or you'll miss your flight."

Stimson smiled. "Relax, Ben. Alison is fine. She came back of her own free will because she loves you. Keep that love strong. You won't lose her."

Ben waved as Pollack drove away.

The rain began to fall harder. Ben hurried to his car and found Alison at the wheel. He signaled through the window for her to slide over, but she refused. He raced around the car and climbed in beside her, his hair drenched. Alison begged him to let her drive. She wanted to feel useful, she said, to feel back in the real world. "Ben, you're being silly," she said when he tried to persuade her to switch places with him. He let the issue drop. He didn't want to pressure her, to make her feel a need to escape. Too many images of death around them invited remembrance.

"I can do it," Alison said. "I've driven in worse weather."

Driving was a test, Ben realized, probably one of many to come by which she'd try to convince him and herself that life had returned to normal.

The sky darkened and suddenly a sheet of rain beat in a solid sound on the roof. Alison let the other cars leave first. She drove slowly along the cemetery path, and by the time she had turned onto the main street she'd regained her confidence behind the wheel. The rain fell solid. The windshield wipers could not move fast enough. Sheets of rain glazed her view of the road. She concentrated harder. When the sky blackened she turned on the headlights. At least now she could see the white line on the road.

Driving was easier on the highway. At a steady forty miles an hour she found that the car's wheels cut smoothly through the water on the road. Traffic was mercifully light. For the last mile she'd seen only one car. Occasionally she'd interject a comment into the conversation, but her concentration was really focused on the road. Ahead was the sharpest curve. She was still too far away to begin slowing down, but she kept the curve in view.

Suddenly she spotted the headlights of a truck rounding the curve. Automatically she tensed. Trucks frightened her and this one was the size of a freight train. The damn idiot! she cursed under her breath. He was taking the curve too wide, hogging the road. She tried to regain her calm. If he didn't pull in soon she'd have to edge out to the berm. She estimated that she had about four to five feet of gravel. Concentrate on the truck, she told herself. There will be room to pass him. The truck's giant headlights blurred in the steady rain and fused into a single light. It shone so brightly against the black sky. Idiot! she wanted to shout. Turn off your high beams! They blinded her. She could see nothing else. She tried to signal the truck, to flash *her* high beams, but her foot would not move to the switch.

"Ali," said Ben, "that jerk's not going to give up the center. Pull out." The truck was uncomfortably close. Coming faster. "Ali, don't wait for him to move. Cut out! Now!" The truck's lights aimed right at them. Ben grabbed Alison's hand. It was ice cold. She was heading for the truck! She was going to kill them!

Seconds remained. With all his force he tried to knock her arms free of the wheel. But they were as rigid as steel. He had to gain control of the car. He tried frantically to pry open her fingers, but her hands were locked to the wheel in a frozen grip. Her strength was incredible! He could not turn the wheel. Not budge it an inch.

They were accelerating! Why was she doing this?

"Ali!" Ben cried desperately, pulling on the wheel with all his strength, "you'll kill us both!" Suddenly he realized what had happened. Alison's eyes were glazed, watery; they reflected the truck's light.

"Ali!" Ben screamed. But she had locked onto the light. They were going to crash. He could do nothing to prevent it. Alison was rushing blindly into the light and taking him with her.